A Wolf in Sheep's Clothing

Queen's Maid Series

Rebecca McIntosh

PRESS

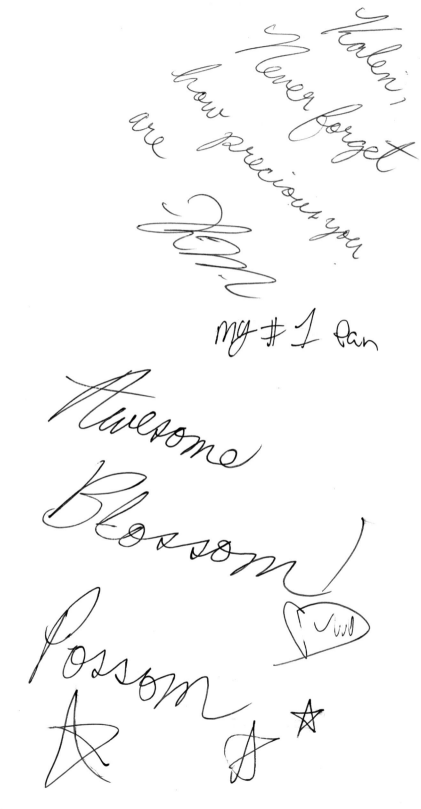

Kaleni,
Never forget
how precious you
are

my #1 fan

Awesome
Blossom
Possom

Table of Contents

1 A New Beginning 7

2 The Queen's Maid....................18

3 New Acquaintances....................31

4 Discoveries 47

5 A Good Sign 64

6 The Ballroom Night....................74

7 Royal Crime....................90

8 In the Wolf's Jaws....................105

9 Weight of Decision 119

10 Jacqueline's Scheme....................132

11 Tests of the Heart 148

12 Moment of Truth....................158

13 Rewarding Results 173

Chapter One

A New Beginning

I have learned that one simple decision can affect the rest of your life. To begin my story, I will travel back two years ago, in the year of our Lord, 1776. This is when my family moved from France to Lydonia. I had lived in France most of my life, but I was not unhappy to leave it. God knows how many hard days my family toiled under persecution and hatred because of our faith. We were despised for bearing the title of Huguenot.

I think my poor Mother had the hardest time of all since my brothers and I were too young to carry heavy responsibilities. While Enrique (my older brother) and I went to school, my elderly grandmother looked after my baby brother, Phillip. Mother would work most of the time, as the town seamstress. While on her errands, she would try to preach the gospel whenever she could.

Where is my father? Well, the honorable and sorely missed Esteban Noble died at sea while serving the Spanish Armada.

My father's legacy is quite interesting. His father, Richard Noble was an Englishman who fell in love with a beautiful Spanish belle, Gabriella Ruiz. Eventually, Grandfather

Richard moved to Spain and there my grandmother birthed Esteban.

As my father grew, he developed a strong desire to serve in the Spanish Armada – for king and country! And so, he did.

One of his travels brought him to France. That's where he met my mother, Genevieve Montelaux. Mother tells me stories of how intriguing and dashingly handsome father was when she first saw him. It was father who drew her to the Lord Jesus Christ. . .and I am so grateful!

Not long after that they were married and settled in Spain. That was where Enrique was born, and finally, me!

After about five years, my parents decided to return to France. We were indeed poor, but we had each other, and most importantly - God.

It was in France that Phillip was born, my mischievous younger brother. Not long after that, three years to be exact, father died at sea. The blow was crushing and it is only by God's amazing grace that we survived. The persecution in France during these years was extremely difficult and mother decided that she didn't want her children growing up in such an oppressive environment. Bidding grandmother farewell, we left France forever.

I was eleven when we moved to the little, yet beautiful country of Lydonia. At least here we were able to worship God in peace. However, our station in life had not improved. My mother was still a poor seamstress and my brothers and I were the children of a poor seamstress.

I remember the day like yesterday. We all walked into our new cottage, which was seated on a hill at the outskirts of Lydonia's capital city, Lyden. The morning dawn was just creeping over the horizon while the dew from the previous night's rain lingered on the grass like tiny gems. The lilac flower dotted the countryside in a lovely array of purple and blue.

My new bedroom is not a real improvement from the last one in France, but it does have a much better view! It looks over the carpets of green hills leading to the town and gives you a glimpse of the royal castle's towers in the far distance. Oh how my heart leaped at such a sight! We were finally home!

I remember kneeling down to pray that night and thanking my heavenly Father for bringing us to such a peaceful place!

Even though the move was a big adjustment, it did little to change my daily life. It wasn't until two years later that I experienced something drastic.

It was late afternoon, and I had just finished gathering the ingredients for a dinner soup. Phillip, who is now five, was pretending to conquer some imaginary villain with his sword - more accurately defined as a small stick. Mother walked in the door, just returning from one of her seamstress errands. "How's dinner coming along Jacqueline?" she said wiping a string of hair from her tired face.

"I haven't got all the ingredients to make the soup," I replied slamming the cabinets with frustration.

"Don't get all upset, you may go to town to get them. I have some money. Here, go."

"But Mother, shouldn't we save this," I replied, always reluctant to spend even the slightest amount of money. "I can make due – I think."

Mother shook her head with a smile, "You needn't worry Jacqueline. Please, take it and go to town."

"Go to town!" my little brother squealed with delight.

I rolled my eyes, knowing what question was coming next.

"May I go to?!"

"Oh Phillip, you have gone to town plenty of times, let me go alone this once!"

"It's not fair! I have just as much of a right to go as you have Jackie! Pleeeease, take me!" he begged going dramatically on his knees and clasping his hands together.

I looked at Mother in desperation. She smiled sympathetically at my little brother's act, "Why don't you let him tag along. It won't take but a few minutes to get the vegetables."

I looked from Mother to Phillip, and then back again. "Fine.

"Yippee!" he shouted.

I slung my brown bag over my shoulder and headed across the lilac fields to the reddish, dirt road leading to Lyden. The soft evening breeze blew through my light brown, wavy curls of hair. It was soothing, and my heart once again became light despite the fact that Phillip was singing a tune at the top of his little five year old lungs while frolicking gaily through the lilacs.

As we neared the huge town, I took hold of Phillip's hand. A little boy could get lost in such a city. Contrary to the quiet countryside on the outskirts of Lyden, the actual town is a constant place of activity and excitement. The royal palace is north of town square. A smooth, neat road leads up to the regal golden gates. I had never ventured far down that road, but gazed at it wonderingly many times.

Phillip and I met a bustle of people from all sizes and ranks as we entered Lyden. The warm summer sun was temporarily blotted out by tall, looming buildings. Unfortunately this gives the prospering city a rather dull appearance.

I moved slowly through the crowd towards the marketplace. Phillip's flamboyant attitude subsided as his big blue eyes took in the sights and people of the town.

Merchants and tradesman from all over Europe station themselves on the side of the streets; calling out to the swarms of people, beckoning, daring them to try some new product or dawn on fancy clothes.

I must admit I do not like these wealth seekers one bit. They are annoying, loud, and full of pride in themselves. With the exception of a few merchants who don't hunt down customers but let the people come to them. One of these people is Mr. Dilamari. He is a Christian and attends the town's Protestant church, Hope Congregation. This tall, large man is very kind and frequently asks how my family is doing.

On this evening, he waved to us from his booth and I waved back. Phillip didn't wave, no that would have been too uncommon for him. Instead my little brother jumped in the air and with a loud voice cried, "Hi Mr. Dilamari!"

Several people turned with annoyed, bewildered, and sometimes amused (that was the worst) faces towards me and my brother. I fervently told him to hold his tongue and to stop leaping up into the air. How embarrassing!

Mr. Dilamari noticed the agitated look on my face and with a chuckle, motioned for us to come on over. I pushed through the people until we were standing right in front of the kindly merchant's displays of fabrics.

"Well, how's my favorite kids today?" he asked with merry eyes.

"Quite well thank you," I replied curtseying.

"We're going to get some vegetables for dinner!" Phillip exclaimed triumphantly.

"Well then, I certainly won't detain you. But on your way back, stop by my shop and I'll give you a surprise."

"Really?!" Phillip exclaimed, his eyes brimming with anticipation. "What are we waitin for! C'mon Jackie, let's get the vegetables!"

I found myself being yanked into the marketplace square. Never have I seen a young boy more eager to find onions, carrots, and all sorts of other greens.

While I was paying for the food, something fluttering in the breeze caught my eye. I turned and saw that it was a large piece of paper nailed to a post. A grand advertisement with beautiful handwriting adorned the parchment. No doubt a prominent person had made it.

"Miss?" the vendor asked as he waited for the money I absently clutched in my right hand.

"Oh, yes, I'm sorry. Here," I said handing him the coins.

"Now let's go to Mr. Dilamari for the surprise!" Phillip said tugging at my skirt.

"In a minute, I want to see something first."

I walked over to a small group of girls who were intent on reading the poster. Intrigued, I began to read for myself. . ."A suitable young woman from the ages of eleven to sixteen is needed to fulfill the service of one of Her Majesty Queen Tabitha's maids. Each young lady who applies will be interviewed on the first and twentieth of May, nine o'clock. The women who want to apply will also kindly gather at the palace's royal gates. . ."

I stopped reading here, for Phillip arrested my attention by tugging ruthlessly on my dress and crying, "C'mon Jackie, let's go!"

"In a minute Phillip!" I glanced once again at the advertisement and memorized the date and time.

You see, I had been considering taking up a job for quite some time and thought with enthusiasm that this might be the answer! Just think, the Queen's maid! Oh I hoped that I'd get the job! "Jacqueline hold your horses, you haven't even told Mother yet," I said to myself; endeavoring to lower my high expectations. But I couldn't suppress a little shimmer of excitement from the hope that it just may happen.

I quickly made my way back to Mr. Dilamari before Phillip had the chance to tear my dress in two.

"Ah, I see you have been so kind as to keep your promise," the merry merchant remarked as we stood in front of him; a little breathless from the mad dash.

"I have a little something for each of you." And from a purple satin box, he uncovered a short piece of scarlet silk fabric; the perfect size for Phillip. "This," he said, "is for you my boy. See, it can be used as a knight's cape or a pirate's head band, whichever you choose."

"Wow, thank you!" Phillip said, receiving the rich piece of cloth with reverent care.

I smiled, "It suits you Phillip."

"And this," Mr. Dilamari added, "is for you Jacqueline."

A beautiful blue silk shawl with lace adorning its hem was laid around my shoulders. I could do nothing but smile from end to end and feel the loveliness cradle me up in its arms. "It's beautiful, thank you," I murmured. "But, why all these wonderful gifts?"

"Oh, I've been meaning to give something to your family since the first time I met you. The shawl is for you and your mother. Take it as thanks for the blueberry pie you sent me."

I made a deep curtsy and thanked him with a full heart

The sun was setting now, and I knew Mother would be worried if we didn't hurry. So hastening across the lilac fields, we made our way back to the cottage. I got dinner ready just in time and was pleased to find the soup didn't taste *that* bad.

Afterwards we all sat down on the knit rug in the living room and Mother opened up the well worn Bible for our daily devotions. Her gentle face glowed in the soft candle-light, "Tonight children," she began, "we will read from the passage of Esther, chapter one. Verse 1 reads. . .Now it came to pass in the days of Ahasuerus, [this is Ahasuerus which reigned from India even unto Ethiopia, over an hundred and seven and twenty provinces] Verse 2 That in those days, when the king Ahasuerus sat on the throne of his kingdom, which was in Shushan the palace, Verse 3 In the third year of his reign, he made a feast unto all his princes and his servants; the power of Persia and Media, the nobles and princes of the provinces, being before him:"

And she went on to tell the story about an extraordinary young woman who was born in poverty during the time of Jewish enslavement under Persia. Esther was beautiful and pleased the king so much that he married her and promoted this virtuous woman to be queen over all the land. Let me tell you, God is a great story maker. I was amazed listening to the first two chapters of Esther's story and how obedient she was to her dear cousin, Mordecai, and how God blessed her so much! Sure I've heard the story many times, but every time God points out something new I've never noticed before.

Mother stopped reading at the end of chapter two and closed the old Bible reverently; placing her hands over it. "Now, is there anything that stuck out to you from these two passages?"

"That the king likes to party!" Phillip exclaimed, a cute smile on his six year old face.

Mother and I laughed.

"No Phillip, she meant is there anything important that you learned from what we read," I clarified.

The little boy placed his soft hand on his chin and knit his eyebrows, pondering deeply. "Well," he began, "God loves Morlicadi. . .

"Mordecai," Mother corrected gently.

"That's what I said, Mordacui. God loves Mordacui and Esther and they are obedient to Jesus."

"That's very good Phillip. Yes they were obedient to Jesus. They didn't question Him when He allowed the guards to take Esther away to the palace. And she turned out to be a queen! What about you Jacqueline?"

"Well, I think it was awfully brave of Esther to accept going to the king's palace, and then become queen. I mean, it must have been a shocker. She also impressed me with how submissive she was to Mordacui," I smiled; imitating Phillips pronunciation.

"Yes, and I hope you will imitate her Jacqueline. Meekness is so often thought of as weakness, when in reality, it is the very thing that makes someone strong. Strong enough to go to the palace, strong enough to accept a crown, and strong enough to face danger, and do the right thing."

"What is meekness Mama?" Phillip asked.

"Meekness is surrendering our hearts to God. Humility also has a tremendous part in this, because it takes humility to surrender to the Lord all our desires and needs. And when we are humble, God pours on us his mighty grace so we can do all things."

We all knelt down to pray after that and then proceeded upstairs to bed. I always thank the Lord he gave me such a wonderful family. They've stayed with me through thick and thin.

I opened my bedroom door and beheld the lovely hue of twilight outside my window. I threw myself onto my bed, and stared out beyond the hills of green to the palace flags far away in the distance.

The advertisement I read in town kept surfacing in my mind.

A soft knock sounded at my door and Mother peeked in.

"Goodnight Jacqueline," she whispered.

I smiled back. Before she closed the door I ventured, "Mother, can I talk to you for a moment?"

"Sure sweetie," she answered. Coming over, she sat on the bed next to me. "What is it?"

I sat up, "Well, you know how you were getting worried that we wouldn't have enough money to send Phillip to school. Well, I've been thinking, what if I got a job? If I did then we would have enough wouldn't we?"

"Oh Jacqueline," she began rather unsteadily, "I. . .I suppose we would. But why are you so eager to start at so young an age?"

"Mom, I'm thirteen! You started working at eleven. Besides, I've done my years of school. A girl isn't expected to go as long as the boys anyway. Since Enrique listed into the Lydonian Military, I don't see why I shouldn't start getting a job now, while I'm still young and able."

My mother gave a little laugh and wry smile, "As opposed to being old and frail like me?"

"No! That's not what I meant," I interjected. A silence enveloped the room as a warm night breeze wafted in from the window.

"Well," Mother said finally, "what did you have in mind?"

That glimmer of excitement once again sparked in my heart. "Today in town I saw an advertisement for the Queen's maid. The interviews for it will take place at nine o'clock tomorrow morning."

"One of the Queen's maids! Darling you sure aim high for one so inexperienced. Are you sure you want to do this?"

"I can't think of a better occupation at this point. Think of it Mother! Me, in the royal castle itself! Well, as one of the humble workers, but it makes no difference!"

Mother smiled, "Be careful Jacqueline. If your motive is just to see the grandness of the Royal Family then I suggest you not do it. Being a maid takes dedication, cheerfulness, and obedience to whatever you are told to do. Do you really think you're up for it?"

I nodded in response, "I certainly want to try."

Mother studied my face for a few minutes. Her eyes softened, "Then you have my permission."

I wrapped my arms around her neck and thanked her. She gave me a kiss, said goodnight, and closed the door.

I was left in the darkness to ponder my decision. Was it wise to do this? What if I failed miserably! Yet what if

I become a great success? Will they even pick me at all? Thoughts swarmed around in my head far into the night. It would be false to say I wasn't nervous or scared. In fact, I was petrified! This would be the first real job I'd ever had.

Silently I closed my eyes and prayed to my Heavenly Father saying, "Dear Lord, please make the jitters in my stomach go down. Just knowing I have them makes me jittery! Father, if you want me to do this job, please, help me do it to the best of my ability. Please pour on me your grace and strength," I paused, "if I don't get the job, please lead me to where you want me to go. Thank you for hearing my prayer, Amen."

God did settle my stomach and I was able to close my eyes and sleep peacefully.

Little did I suspect that this was the start of a new life filled with adventure I never dared to dream of.

Chapter Two

The Queen's Maid

*T*he sun rose in all its morning glory over the lush hills sparkling with dew. I sat up in my bed and yawned long and hard. The thought suddenly came to me that my first job interview was today!

A knot of uncertainty and excitement formed in my stomach; giving me a rush of energy to sprint downstairs and eat breakfast. Did I say eat? I meant pick at. The other result of having a stomach infested with butterflies is that you usually can't swallow a thing.

"Nervous Jacqueline?" Mother commented with a slight smile.

I straightened up, "Not at all."

"Then why won't you eat?" Phillip asked taking a huge bite out of his bread.

"Because, I'm. . .just not that hungry." A lame excuse.

The time ticked by slowly and I went around the cottage doing my chores at lightning speed. Why wouldn't time just hurry up! I'd rather face the interview now then go through this agonizing wait.

Phillip gave me puzzled expressions as I fluttered around like a nervous humming bird. I had to keep reminding myself that I might not even get the job, and shouldn't be so anxious. Easier said then done.

Finally, it was time.

Mother wished me well and kissed my forehead. Phillip saluted me in his red cape and I ventured forward into the world, unsure and at the same time strangely confident.

A beautiful breeze swirled around the hills and for the first time, I found myself disliking it. I had brushed my hair especially well this morning and I was vexed as the wind threatened to undue my efforts.

I walked along the road leading to the town and felt my heart skip a beat as I neared the looming buildings. The stomach butterflies started acting up again and I had no power to control them!

I said a frantic prayer to God, "Jesus, pleeease help me!"

As I neared the town's main square I became really nervous. The road leading to the royal gates started here. For a moment I hesitated. Doubts started clouding my mind once again.

"Go," commanded a steady voice inside me.

Setting my jaw in resolution, I strode down the road of destiny.

The morning's sun glinted on two golden objects in the distance.

"The gates!" I thought triumphantly. I found myself walking at a faster pace just as I noticed a group of young women gathered at the base of the grand entrance. They were all talking at once in hushed, excited tones. Near this feminine company was a long line. At the far end of the line sat a very plump woman behind a wooden desk trying to sort out names and ages on a parchment.

I slowly made my way through the fluttering group of girls to the waiting line.

My anxiety quickly gave place to a feeling of grand excitement. I drummed my fingers on my thigh in anticipation. My eyes traveled beyond the golden gates to the palace behind them. My sense of curiosity is strong, and I couldn't help imagining what it would be like to explore such a mysterious and wonderful place.

A slight shuffle behind me made my gazing eyes turn around. I saw a young girl, no older than I, take her place in line. She had black glossy hair, olive skin, and finely shaped oriental eyes. I gave her a friendly smile and she nodded with civility.

The tall blond in front of me finished reciting her age and name so I stepped up to the desk.

"Name and age please," the plump women recited with a sigh that manifested her boredom.

"Jacqueline Noble, age thirteen!" I said enthusiastically.

"And have you ever been a maid before?"

"No, ma'm," I replied somewhat less confidently.

"Step to the side," the lady pointed with her quill pen.

I did so with haste and made way for the oriental girl. She stepped up directly to the desk and repeated the same ritual.

As I watched her, it suddenly struck me that this girl was certainly no amateur. Her whole demeanor held neither agitation nor excitement. She appeared perfectly calm, which stirred surprise, admiration, and irritation inside me. Why couldn't I be that serene?

The girl walked off to the side and sat on the grass as the next young lady stepped up.

I don't know why she interested me, but I continued to study her. She was not of an aristocratic family - her clothes testified to it. However, she didn't seem extremely poor either. I watched her dark, brown eyes gaze longingly at the crowd of girls.

It was in that moment that I realized she was lonely; compassion quickly filled my heart.

Acting on impulse, I made my way over to her. I didn't want to make her uncomfortable, so I tried to appear nonchalant by examining the castle through the tall, golden fence.

I sat down on the grass near her. Trying to make conversation I stated, "Isn't it a beautiful structure."

It took a second for the girl to realize I directed the remark toward her. "Oh yes, quite magnificent."

I nodded. "Well, this is awkward," I thought, "attempting to make conversation with a girl who apparently doesn't want it."

I started pulling the grass and playing with it.

The girl glanced at me sheepishly and remarked, "So, this is your first job."

I looked up, "Yes, it is. And you?"

"I've never interviewed for such a position like this. But I'm used to interviews."

"So you've had jobs before?"

She nodded, "Yes. My father and I moved here from China eleven years ago. We needed something to stand on, so, when I was of age I started working."

I smiled, quite impressed, "Well then, perhaps you can give me some tips because I have never had a job before. My mother wanted me to go to school first."

"Experience is the best teacher," the girl said smiling slightly.

"In this case, you are wiser than me," I laughed.

She gave me a big smile, "My name is Lin Chang."

"I'm Jacqueline Noble," I replied extending my hand.

Lin shook it and a glimmer of light came into her eyes.

"Alright ladies line up!" the stout woman commanded as she rose from behind the desk. "Miss Hilda Primpette will be inspecting you in a moment and I want all to express their best behavior. Miss Primpette is the Head Supervisor of all female maids in the royal palace."

Lin and I stood side by side in line and waited for this highly esteemed lady to arrive. I'll never forget the first time I beheld Miss Hilda Primpette. One could not miss her in a crowd for she was a very tall lady; with a decided air, prominent jaw, smoothly arched eyebrows, and sharp green eyes which furthered her critical nature. Miss Primpette's flowing gown was fine but practical, while her fluffy cinnamon hair sat high on her head.

How did I feel when I saw her? In one word – intimidated.

The nervous, fluttery feeling in my stomach returned, this time with more intensity as I stood in the heat of the situation. I clasped my hands behind my back and took a fleeting glance at Lin. Her face looked tense, but I could see she was controlling herself well.

Miss Primpette took a long, keen glance at the line of young girls. Then she slowly paraded down the line.

As Miss Primpette turned her eyes at me, she raised a critical eyebrow.

My eyes fell to the ground as her penetrating gaze scanned me up and down. I felt as if my every flaw was glowing in the sunlight for all to see. My cheeks started to burn.

A feeling of relief swept over me when the lady proceeded down the line. I took another glance at Lin. She had bit her lower lip and was staring straightforward.

When Miss Primpette was satisfied with our inspection she joined the stout woman in front of us. "The Great Queen Tabitha is in need of only two maids," Miss Primpette declared. "Therefore I will give two of you a week's trial to prove your worth. However, it is the Queen who will ultimately decide if you remain under her service. So, the two girls I choose will be wise to gain Her Majesty's favor – by hard work."

My hands became sweaty in anticipation for what I knew was coming next.

"I will take her and her," the lady pointed.

Was I dreaming or did that finger point at me? Yes! It did! You can't believe the surprise and delight that all of a sudden numbed my senses!

"Step forward!" the stout woman bellowed.

I did so as if in a trance, when suddenly I found Lin standing right next to me.

We had been chosen together!

Miss Primpette did not seem as exhilarated, and dismissed the rest of the group without ceremony. Lin and I were the only ones who stayed.

I looked at my companion and smiled, "Well, it looks like we'll be seeing each other a lot."

Lin grinned, "Then I suppose our meeting was no accident."

"Yeah, God definitely planned it," I replied.

She looked at me with a queer expression.

All of a sudden a feeling of awkwardness came over me as I realized (like I should be surprised) that Lin was not a Christian. My mind raced back to France. The tormenting persecution my family and I endured for so many years surfaced in my thoughts. Lin didn't seem the type to laugh at me for strange ideas but still, I realized our friendship was going to be hard to maintain.

Miss Primpette's commanding voice arrested my attention, "Miss Noble and Miss Chang, you have a very difficult task ahead of you that is not to be taken lightly." She bent down and looked us straight in the eye, "I will be watching you."

I gulped.

Miss Primpette straightened up and gathered her fancy shawl around her shoulders, "I will expect both of you to be here crisp and early tomorrow, shall we say, five o'clock."

"Five o'clock!" I screamed within myself. "Absolutely," I replied curtseying.

Lin did the same.

As I trudged back home that evening, mixed emotions of joy and fear enveloped my soul. Yes! I got the job! But can I do it? The thought of meeting the Queen of Lydonia excited and frightened me. Then there was Lin. Would our friendly acquaintance last?

All these thoughts eventually gave me a headache. "Oh I don't know what to think!" I cried to the lilac hills. My mind was in a daze.

The setting sun painted the skies above with pastel hues. I closed my eyes and breathed in the fresh air. When my eyes opened, I saw two bluebirds fluttering together, chirping a lovely song. It brought a scripture verse to my mind. . .Mathew 1:26-27, "Behold the fowls of the air: for they sow not, neither do they reap, nor gather into barns; yet your heavenly Father feedeth them. Are ye not much better than they? Verse 27 Which of you by taking thought can add one cubit unto his stature?"

I smiled to myself, "God, you know just what I need. Alright, I'll stop worrying."

"Wake up Jackiiieeee!" Phillip's voice yelled in my ear.

I could feel the bed shake as he pounced on me. I opened my eyes groggily and stared at my bright faced brother. I gave him a look of disdain and flopped the pillows over my head, "Go away!"

"You wouldn't say that to your bruther Jackie?" he moaned in fake misery. "Besides, don't you have to go to the cawstle?"

All of a sudden I wasn't tired anymore but jumped out of bed; nearly engulfing Phillip with a wave of sheets. I looked frantically out the window and was relieved to find that dawn was still not ahead of me. "I have to get ready," I murmured going to my dress closet.

Phillip's head popped out of the tussled sheets, "Aren't you glad I woke you up?!"

I turned around to face him. Putting my hands on my hips I was ready to give him a scolding, but the look of bright sincerity in his face made me say, "Yes, I suppose so."

This satisfied him and he bounded out of the room.

I dawned on my sandy colored dress and tied my wavy curls of hair up into a bun. I wasn't going to the castle for tea, but for work.

The morning sun was creeping over the horizon and the faint twitter of birds could be heard in the swaying willow trees. I only wished my heart would be as peaceful as my surroundings. The wooden stairs creaked as I made my way to the table for breakfast. Mother had already laid out fresh fruit for me to eat and a cup of milk. She was sitting in a rocking chair near the fire, reading the Bible.

When I sat down at the table she looked up and smiled, "Good morning dear. Did you sleep well?"

"I could have slept better," I commented, giving Phillip a brief look.

Mother smiled and joined me at the table. "I want you to know that I am very proud of you. I know you'll do well."

I looked up from my apple into her gentle face, "Thanks Mother."

She kissed me on the forehead and then went to help Phillip who had just shouted from upstairs that he couldn't find his trousers.

I devoured my breakfast then took my brown bag and once again slung it over my shoulder. I opened the cottage door and crept out into the morning twilight. Everything was so still and quiet. A fresh mist hung in the air as I walked across the rolling green hills leading to the town. I picked a few lilacs along the way, hoping to give some to Lin.

The usually bustling entrance to Lyden was now very mellow. No carriages whisked by, no vendors debated with customers, and no merchants cried out their products to the people. The high buildings only shadowed a few scattered peasants here and there. I made my way to the fountain in the center of town and once again followed the cobblestone road to the castle.

By now the sun's rays were almost over the hills and in its beam of light, I saw the royal palace, in all splendor and glory. It took my breath away! The light was hitting it just right and made it more enchanting than a heavenly fairytale. I took in a deep breath and smiled as I proceeded down the road.

I foresaw Lin waiting at the Golden Gates. When she caught sight of me down the road she waved.

"Hi Lin! Is Miss Primpette here yet?" I greeted.

She shook her head, "I think the grand Miss Primpette should be here any moment."

I smiled, "So the mistress is not as prompt as she seems. . ."

"Good morning ladies," Miss Primpette interrupted. As if by magic, she suddenly appeared striding up to us with an air of authority.

I bit my lower lip and curtseyed with Lin. "What perfect timing," I thought uneasily.

"If you two will just follow me," Miss Primpette directed; turning around and heading east around the castle's tall, beautiful fence.

We came around to an arched gateway. We paused as a steady stream of palace servants were passing through a pair of rich, wooden doors. Two guards, yawning as they came, posted themselves at the entrance just as we neared it.

"This," Miss Primpette explained, "is the servants' entranceway and you will enter here when you come to work tomorrow."

Both guards saluted when the lady walked through. We entered a small courtyard with lovely flowers and trees surrounding it on both sides. At the other end was the castle itself; and three separate doors leading inside!

I tilted my head high to see the end of the palace towers and gazed in awe at its incredible outward beauty and magnificent size.

"Keep up girls! We can't have Her Majesty waiting!" Miss Primpette squawked.

I walked at a faster pace and came in step with Lin.

"This is so awesome!" I whispered.

Lin nodded quietly, "I've never seen such a spectacular place as this."

I looked at her face and noted an expression of intimidation in it. Half smiling I looped my arm with hers and presented the lilac flowers, "Well, now we've seen everything. We'll never have to travel again!"

Lin smiled and received the flowers with thanks.

We neared a doorway and ascended up a set of stairs. At the top, we entered a great hall with marble floors and enormous white pillars with a breathtaking crystal chandelier hanging from the ceiling. Beautiful plants graced the spacious area and glass statues of dramatic women were placed around the hall with artistic design. Off to the left, a doorway displayed a richly decorated sitting room; with stylish sofas, lavish furniture, graceful draping curtains, and large windows revealing floral gardens.

I could feel my eyes getting brighter and bigger as I took in these heavenly attributes. Down farther to the right, there was a corridor leading to some sort of lovely veranda. Straight ahead was a doorway opening up into a marvelous dining room. There were many other rooms leading off from this enormous hall but their doors were closed and therefore, remained a mystery.

Centered in the hall was a white, long, extensive, staircase. Its railings consisted of stunning, intricate, golden designs and at its posts sat two graceful, stone Pegasus.

"I feel like I'm walking in a dream," Lin remarked in awe.

I caught Miss Primpette watching us with amused expressions as we soaked in the splendor of the castle's east wing. Somewhat annoyed by the lady's lofty air, I straightened my back and appeared to be less impressed.

"This wing is the Queen's private area. No one is allowed in this section of the palace except the royal family and Her Majesty's personal maids. And me of course," Miss Primpette added.

We were led up the snowy white staircase to a corridor that encircled the entire area of the downstairs. Four royal doors were stationed in this circle; one being Her Majesty's bedroom, another was the clothing room, the other a powder room, and the fourth a drawing room.

Miss Primpette took us to the bedroom first. With a slight knock an older maid opened the door.

"Miss Primpette," the maid said curtseying deeply, "Queen Tabitha is expecting you. She is taking a bath right now but she won't be long."

"I thought she would be ready. Everything is alright I presume?"

"Oh yes, quite. It's simply the preparations for the ball that is tiring her. And of course the usual. . ." the maid stopped here, letting her tone suggest something. Miss Primpette seemed to understand completely and nodded her head in response.

The elderly maid closed the door and Miss Primpette turned to us, "Well ladies, it looks like we'll have to wait. In the meantime, I think it would be prudent to dress yourselves in uniform."

Lin and I exchanged a look of perplexity.

It was then I noticed that Miss Primpette took pleasure from knowing more than the people around her. In answer to our puzzled expressions she merely raised a proud eyebrow and stated, "Follow me."

We were led back downstairs to a corner room. It was quite small and consisted of a few cleaning tools and two sets of clothes. Miss Primpette took these outfits and placed them in our arms. "These are your new work clothes. They are the official dress of the queen's maids. Wear them with dignity."

"And where are we to change madam?" I asked.

"I don't care! Just be ready so I can to present you to the Queen – whenever that may be!"

Well, Lin and I took turns changing in the closet. The 'uniform' as Miss Primpette so called it, was actually very nice. I don't mean to say it was a ball gown but it certainly looked better than what I had on before. Its main color was a deep blue, with a white lace apron in front. As I finished adjusting the neckline, a tingle of exhilaration shivered through my veins. Now, I really felt like a maid! Being dressed up for a job certainly encouraged my confidence!

I immerged from the closet with renewed energy and anticipation. It may not seem a big deal to you reader, but for me, it was a stepping stone. I had now transferred from child to young adult. I now possessed my own job, and was going to help support my family.

Miss Primpette stood in the grand hall; hands clasped in front of her and eyes darting about with impatience.

I looked at Lin and whispered, "The color suits you."

She smiled, "I rather think it fits you better. It compliments your blue eyes."

I tried to brush aside the compliment, "Thanks."

Lin gave a little giggle as she observed Miss Primpette, "A bit of hair flattening would do her good. I dare say she's half the height she appears to be."

I smiled and whispered back, "Yeah, not to mention those haughty, high eyebrows."

This time Lin's giggle was just enough for the lady to hear. Miss Primpette turned sharply towards us; eyes flashing with suspicion.

Lin and I looked at the ground and bit our lips with suppressed merriment.

During this moment, the elderly maid mentioned earlier, came down the white staircase.

With the air of a solemn propriety she said, "The Queen is ready to see you now."

Chapter Three

New Acquaintances

*W*e were shown once again to Her Majesty's private quarters – to be specific, the drawing room.

The elderly maid opened the door promptly and said in a gracious tone, "Your Majesty, Miss Primpette."

The maid stepped aside and allowed us to enter.

I can never forget the day I met the Queen! I entered the lovely drawing room with glowing expectation. The room possessed all the delicious qualities of a home, yet at the same time displayed all of the new, rich fashions. Lace white curtains swayed gracefully as a light morning breeze blew through the air. The walls were of a soft, flowery blue design and accentuated the dark cherry furniture. A ring of plush sofas surrounded an elegant table; which was draped with lace and adorned with a beautiful vase of soft lilac flowers. A grand, golden harp stood gracefully in one corner while breathtaking, artistic paintings hung on the walls.

All of this caught my attention only for a moment; and then, my eyes beheld *her*.

Queen Tabitha sat with regal grace upon one of the plush sofas near the window. I supposed her age to be about forty five. Her physical features were not exquisitely beautiful, as one might expect, rather they were plain, and sensible; with the exception that her cheeks and lips were painted and her face powdered. Her white wig was adorned with strings of pearls and her dress announced quite plainly that she was a Queen – a wealthy one too. Her expression was not one of arrogance or pride, but of grace and dignity. She appeared to have a mild, gentle disposition. However, first impressions so rarely give the whole picture of a person's character.

"My Queen," Miss Primpette curtseyed deeply.

Lin and I did the same.

The honor I felt to be in the presence of one as great as the Queen of Lydonia is truly hard to describe!

Her Majesty acknowledged our reverence with a nod and a pleasant smile. With an elegant gesture the Queen said, "Please, sit down if you will."

"That will be unnecessary Your Highness, for I am needed elsewhere very soon. However, I desired the plea-sure of introducing your two new maids - Jacqueline Noble and Lin Chang."

I felt my knees become wobbly as I nervously curtseyed again.

"I kept my promise and got young girls for you. They are capable of performing any task you wish. They are young, hardy, and I hope, will not disappoint you." Miss Primpette emphasized the last sentence with a glaring look at us.

"I'm sure they will do fine," the Queen replied casually.

"Very well then, if there is nothing else, I shall be on my way," Miss Primpette said with a quick curtsey and walked out the door.

A very awkward silence enveloped the room as Lin and I stood quietly before Her Ladyship. I looked slightly over at my companion. Lin didn't seem as agitated like I was. Then again, she had an art for holding her countenance well.

"Perhaps she is pretending to be calm and meek," I said to myself. However, I couldn't stand so still and my hands began fiddling with my apron.

The Queen must have noticed this for she smiled and compassionately said, "Please, don't feel ill at ease. I am not as dreadful as I seem. I am very pleased that you two have come to work for me. You seem capable of meeting my demands so we shall get along quite well."

Addressing herself to the old maid, Her Majesty continued, "Edna, show these girls what their morning duties will require. I need peace while I can get it."

For the first time, I noticed that the eyes of Her Majesty appeared very weary indeed. She looked stressed, as if a heavy burden were upon her shoulders.

Edna nodded respectfully and proceeded to usher us out of the room.

Just as we were about to leave, two finely dressed young ladies whirled into the scene and began to talk suddenly with the Queen.

Lin and I exchanged surprised expressions.

"Queen Tabitha," curtseyed the first, "we have come back to inform you that King Gilbert will be conversing with the Council and will not be able to join you for lunch."

I saw the Queen's eyes flash a brief icy look. "And my daughter?" she asked.

"The Princess refuses and says she is going out with her friends."

The Queen turned sharply back to them and demanded, "Which friends?"

The two young women gave each other a knowing look, "The Prime Minister's daughters. The Latone Sisters of course."

I saw the Queen grimace in disgust, "Such stupid, silly company! I thought I instructed her never to go out with them again! Does she not remember?! Oh why am I even

asking, of course she remembers! Rebellious girl! Tell her
that all royal carriages are no longer at her disposal and she
must dine with me."

The young ladies nodded their assent vigorously,
"Absolutely! No demand could be better! Her Majesty is
beautifully prudent!"

The Queen heard their comments with irritation.
Presently, Her Highness's eyes fell on us.

Edna immediately began hurrying us out of the room.
Clearly, the old maid thought we had seen enough.

"Oh please, don't leave yet," the Queen stated. "Let me
introduce you to my Ladies in Waiting. They have been doing
a few personal assignments for me. The eldest is Charlotte
Marge and this is Kelsey Barnes."

Both girls looked at us with affected warmth and immediately returned their attention to the Queen.

Edna rushed us out of the room and down the grand
white staircase.

It appeared to me that the old maid was simply tol-
erating us; for she hastily handed me a slip of paper with
assignments and then happily walked away.

Lin and I were left alone in the echoing hall.

"Well," I began after some time, "it looks like we're going
to have to do things ourselves."

I studied the piece of paper meticulously. Lin did the
same while looking over my shoulder.

"It seems," she said after reading it, "that there are an
even number of chores. I suggest we split them between
ourselves. It would make things easier."

"Yes, good idea." I ripped the paper in two and gave
one half to Lin. "But," I paused, "the rooms are very big.
Shouldn't we do this together?"

Lin looked up at me, "Only if you want to. It would be
nicer than spending the whole day cleaning alone."

I smiled, "So we are friends then?"

Lin grinned in return and offered her hand, "Friends."
I took it warmly and we walked together into the first
large room.

It is impossible to describe the grand rooms we cleaned
except to state that they were nothing short of a heavenly
fairytale! Cleaning them, however, was another story. With
a lot of space comes a lot of cleaning – and there was *tons*
of space. To dust every corner, and polish every floor is no
easy task! Don't get the wrong impression that only Lin and I were
working tirelessly. No, there were several other maids as
well. But since Lin and I didn't know them, we stuck together.

We worked side by side and inevitably began to find
out more about each other. Both of us groaned at the same
things, laughed at one another for silly mistakes and talked
about everything. It made the work lighter and helped us
pass the time in a more enjoyable way.

As we began to dust the library, Lin started a new topic
of conversation by asking, "So, what is your opinion of
Queen Tabitha?"

I replaced the dusted items back on the shelf, "Well,
there's not much I can say from just one meeting. But, I will
say that she seems gracious enough. . .and perhaps a little
stressed."

"A little?" Lin added with a lifted brow.

I smiled, "She also struck me as a woman who doesn't
seem to know how to use her power."

"What do you mean?"

"Well, you noticed the way she talked about her
daughter."

Lin grinned and quoted, "A rebellious girl!"

"Yes, and don't you think that a wise Queen would train
her daughter to act the way a princess should act – good
and obedient."

Lin shrugged, "Perhaps, but it must be hard to be a princess. Think of all the things you're not allowed to do. Perhaps Princess Vanessa is just trying to get some freedom."

I gave a small laugh, "I can't see how going against the Queen's wishes would give someone freedom. Wouldn't it just tighten her grip?"

Lin paused, "Yes, I suppose your right. Well then, the Princess better watch out."

After a few minutes, Lin asked another question, "Do you like the Ladies in Waiting?"

"Not at all," I replied stoutly.

Lin laughed, "Why on earth not?"

"I'm not sure. They appear to be quite jealous for the Queen's attention and I'm convinced that if anybody got in their way – boy would that person be sorry!"

Lin couldn't help laughing at my answer, "You seem to be quite a judge of character. What was your opinion when you met me?"

"A very smart girl who needed a friend," I replied with a smile.

She half smiled but appeared nervous to meet my gaze. The gesture was small, but not insignificant. I wondered what she was thinking and waited for a reply, but none came.

Silence washed over the room.

All of a sudden an idea sprang up from my heart, "Why don't I ask Lin to come to church?!"

Another voice argued inside me, "No! What if she thinks your weird and flat out refuses?!"

"Well you'll never know unless you ask," the other replied.

"She's your friend, you wouldn't want to offend her would you?" shot back the other voice.

A sudden uneasiness entered my soul as I debated what to do. I knew I should ask her to church, but I didn't want to face the pang of rejection if she called me weird and refused.

"Blessed is he who shall not be offended in Me," a still voice reminded. Those were the words of Jesus. "Jesus was rejected everywhere he went," I murmured, "that didn't stop him." A wave of guilt swept over me. What would I do if Lin never accepted Christ and went to hell!

This was enough motivation for me to blurt out, "Lin, do you want to come with me to church on Sunday?"

She looked up, quite surprised at my sudden voice. "Uh, well, what is church?"

I sighed with relief and said to myself, "Well, that response was better than 'no way loser!'"

Lin waited for a reply.

"Well, church is a place where Christians worship God. We also go there to hear a pastor preach from the Bible."

Lin looked puzzled, "What are Christians? And what is the Bible? Is this a religious thing?"

I gulped at the tone of her voice. "It is more than just a religion. Christianity is a word describing a person's intimate relationship with Jesus Christ."

Lin looked very skeptical, "I don't know who you're talking about? Who is Jesus?"

I bit my lip. How was I to explain this to her? I decided to describe it to her the way my older brother, Enrique, had told me. "Jesus is the Son of God; who created everything! The earth, the seas, the skies, the universe! He even made us."

"Us?"

"Yes, you and me. But we sin against God Lin, and when we do that, we separate ourselves from Him. There is a being out there called the Devil, who is the sworn enemy of God and our souls. He wants us desperately not to realize what we've done and suffer the consequences of opposing God - death."

Lin sniffed, "Well, isn't that a nice story. So there's no hope and we all die."

"No! God wouldn't dream of leaving us without a hope! That's where Jesus comes in!" I had hardly realized how excited I was getting. "Even though we broke God's heart in disobeying him, he decided to send His only begotten Son, Jesus, to come down here and die for our sins! Jesus led a blameless, perfect life, trying telling people that He was their hope and salvation. But, instead of accepting him, we crucified him on a cross."

Lin's eyes were wide, either from interest or surprise at my mounting energy. "I still don't see how that is hopeful. He died."

A smile split my face, "But He didn't stay dead. After three days in the tomb, Jesus Christ rose from the dead! He conquered death and now sits at the right hand of God the Father! Now, whoever confesses with their mouth that Jesus is Lord and believes in their heart that God raised him from the dead, they shall be saved from the same fate as the Devil." I stopped and took a breath.

Lin stared at me with a look I couldn't make out.

Realizing what I had just said, and the energy that had accompanied it, I bit my lip in astonishment. Did I just do what I think I did? I shared the salvation message! A feeling of delight and amazement overcame my soul such as I had never felt before! I looked back at Lin and held my breath for her answer.

She had resumed cleaning and replied in a casual tone, "I'll think about coming to church."

I quietly breathed a sigh of relief. It wasn't a positive answer, but it was hopeful. A very awkward silence followed Lin's reply. Trying to lighten up the atmosphere I asked, "So, what do you think of Edna?"

Lin smiled, "I think she's old and selfish, not to mention terrible with children."

"It certainly did seem like she wanted to be rid of us," I commented.

Just then, Edna walked into the room. Both of us quickly became quiet as we finished dusting.

I couldn't help grinning at the elderly maid's timely entrance.

Edna walked briskly over to me and instructed, "Queen Tabitha is in need of a bouquet of fresh flowers for her tea table. Go to the garden and fetch some."

I nodded meekly and entered the great hall, proceeding towards the veranda.

The afternoon sun shone gloriously as I beheld a vast sea of flowery gardens. This garden was merely one of a series that extended the entire length of the palace. To see all of the beautiful colors nearly took my breath away!

You can imagine how difficult it was to select the perfect bouquet for Her Highness.

As I ventured farther into this fairyland it became even harder to choose! Eventually I came upon a lovely path over-shadowed by graceful willow trees. It was such a romantic scene! Soft breezes rustling through the leaves of draping willow trees, birds twittering, soft flowers doting the grass and the soothing sound of water bubbling out of a nearby fountain.

"Oh! How gorgeous this place must be at twilight!" I murmured dreamily.

At this moment a whistling tune reached my ears and it quickly brought me back to reality.

I turned my head and saw that the source of the charming melody was a gardener gently tending some lilacs. He was an elderly man with a sun burnt face, grey hair, and soiled hands. After a few minutes he stopped whistling and wiped his sweaty forehead. Catching sight of me he smiled and waved. His smile and blue eyes were some of the kindest I have ever seen.

I repeated his salutation just as he said, "How are you this afternoon my dear?"

"Quite well thank you," I replied politely. "However, I am having a hard time deciding which flowers to give to Her Majesty the Queen."

"I think I can help with that. You see those red roses over there to the left. Well, those are Queen Tabitha's favorite."

"Thank you!" I exclaimed rushing towards the lush plants.

"Don't pick them!" the gardener warned.

I stopped dead in my tracks.

The man made his way over to me and slipped on a pair of thick gloves, "These roses have thorns on them. I wouldn't want you getting hurt, let me pick them."

"Thank you again sir," I said stepping back.

When he had finished cutting the prickles off of the flowers, he handed them to me and studied my face. "I believe I've seen you before!" he declared. "Do you attend Hope Congregation Church?"

"I do!" I replied enthusiastically.

He smiled, "Well so do I. The name's Frank Fairday!" he declared shaking my hand warmly.

I blinked a couple of times with delight, "Hi, I'm Jacqueline Noble."

"It is very nice to meet you Jacqueline. You have just become one of the Queen's maids?"

"Yes, my trial period starts today. Miss Primpette will see if I qualify for the job. Only the best is allowed by Miss Primpette."

Mr. Fairday nodded his head in understanding.

We were quiet for a few minutes and the peaceful sounds of the gardens once again surrounded me.

"I have been here for a long time Jacqueline, and God has preserved me. You will learn to live with the interesting characters that make up this establishment."

"I have met quite a few already."

Mr. Fairday's eyes twinkled, "You will meet more. Good day Miss Noble." And with a slight bow, he returned to his work.

I nodded in return and made my way back to the castle. To me, Mr. Fairday seemed almost angelic. I felt like I could have talked with him more and I was disappointed to get back to work – who wouldn't be?

Approaching the elegant veranda, I beheld the Queen sitting in a lavish white seat while her Ladies in Waiting stood by her protectively. In front of Her Majesty sat a beautiful pink and white lace tea table set with cookies and crumpets. A glass vase stood in the center, waiting for the roses I had picked. Trying not to draw attention I quickly placed the flowers in the lovely container and was hurrying away when the Queen's voice said, "Oh maid! Yes you, Ja. . .Julianne?"

"Jacqueline," I corrected.

The Queen smiled, "Forgive me Jacqueline, but could you go to the kitchen and get the tea? Vanessa will be here any minute."

"Yes madam," I curtseyed and entered the great hall without a clue as to where I would find tea. I assumed that the tea was in the kitchen but. . .I didn't know where the kitchen was! Looking frantically about me I spotted Edna.

"Edna! Edna! Hi, can you tell me where the kitchen is?"

With irritation Edna replied, "What do you need the kitchen for?"

"Queen Tabitha would like her tea," I answered with a hint of annoyance at her sappy attitude. I looked down and saw that the elderly maid was carrying the tray of tea herself.

With a twisted grin Edna put the tray in my hands, "Well then, if the Queen wanted you to give it to her, take it!" And wiping her hands with satisfaction, the maid left me.

"Old hag," I murmured to myself. I made my way back to the veranda and placed the tray of tea on the table.

"Thank you Jacqueline!" the Queen exclaimed with delight. "Now could you get those napkins over there?" Her Majesty pointed to the far end of the veranda.

I nodded and obeyed. Just as I was setting the lovely napkins in place, Miss Primpette entered the scene and announced, "Your Highness, I have brought you Princess Vanessa and her Ladies in Waiting!"

I looked up with keen curiosity.

A young girl, about my age, walked out onto the veranda with two older women behind her. The two older women seemed to anticipate the younger one's every wish and they watched her constantly.

"Those must be the Ladies in Waiting," I concluded.

Then my gaze focused on the Princess. I was quite astonished at her stunning beauty. Her skin was a soft, peach pearl hue and her plump lips the color of a pale rose. Her black, glossy hair was styled into a bun while ringlets cascaded onto her creamy shoulders. Sparkling diamonds adored her neck, wrists and ears. She wore a flowing, sky blue, satin gown that graciously swept across the floor. The Princess' hazel, haughty eyes and finely arched eyebrows betrayed a stubborn, opinionated nature.

I immediately felt ill at ease in her presence. I dropped a napkin on the floor and stooped down to pick it up.

"Welcome dear," the Queen invited her daughter.

Princess Vanessa sat down reluctantly and began, "I don't understand why you insisted that I dine with you. There is nothing wrong with the Latone Sisters! You are just upset because they aren't boring, perfect tempered angels! I declare, they know how to have a jollier time than you!"

"Oh I have no doubt they have merry times - for now. But when they get older they will be stupid, spoiled girls," the Queen stated taking a sip of tea.

"You are so rude I shall never forgive you!" the Princess cried. "What can be the harm of shopping and attending a couple of dances everyday with them?!"

"I let you do those things, just not with them. The reason is that they buy stuff they don't even want while shopping, and flirt up a storm at dances. It's scandalous! Mr. Latone may not want to uphold a good reputation but I do! I will not have the country of Lydonia disgraced because Princess Vanessa made a spectacle of herself."

"So you just don't want our reputation marred, is that it?" questioned the Princess.

"Well, if you manage *that* I shall be very pleased," the Queen replied.

They both became silent for some time. I could see the Queen was thoroughly tired with her daughter and wanted peace.

After a while, Queen Tabitha spoke soothingly, "Let us not talk about it anymore dear. Tell me what you want to do for the ball."

The Princess seemed delighted to tell all about her ideas and opinions. She talked on in raptures about dresses, jewelry, shoes, the people who were going to attend the ball (especially the rich young men) and everything else! It took a while for her to realize that her tea cup was not filled. When the realization did dawn on Her Highness, she became furious.

"Someone please fill my tea cup! Goodness gracious! Who are the dumb maids that work for you mother?!"

I colored and looked at the Queen for some support as I began to pour the tea.

The Queen appeared undisturbed and replied in an indifferent tone, "Now darling, don't refer to the maids that way."

Her Majesty's answer didn't satisfy me at all, in fact, it was insulting! As I poured the tea into the Princess' cup, I bit my lip in an effort not to say something defensive. However, as I lifted the teapot, I failed to notice the few droplets of tea spilling onto the Princess's lovely blue gown.

I may not have realized it, but *she* did. Princess Vanessa let out a startling scream!

"Look what you've done!" she cried in agony looking at the spot.

"I'm terribly sorry. . .I didn't mean to. . ." I fumbled awkwardly, but the Princess interrupted me. . .

"You stupid, senseless girl! You. . .you! What is your name?!" she demanded.

"Jacqueline Noble," I stated, trying to sound immune to her insults.

"That name sounds far too high for a girl of such low rank!" she replied spitefully. Then with a mischievous smile she added, "I think I'll change your name to the Jack Maid. It suits you."

I still don't know how I held my tongue after that. It must have been divine intervention because I was fully prepared to spit out some awful comments. I felt my cheeks grow hot at the burning humiliation!

I turned quickly to the Queen and quietly asked if there was anything else she needed.

"No dear, that will be all. In fact, why don't you take a break," the Queen said with a look of pity that held a hint of condescension. Unfortunately, this deepened my embarrassment further than her daughter's insults. I knew Her Majesty meant well, but I would have preferred her to reprove the Princess for her behavior.

I turned and strutted out the door, but not without catching Miss Primpette's eye. She looked down at me with obvious displeasure.

"Oh no! Now she'll never let me keep this job, and all because of an accident!" I thought to myself. That was the last straw! I hurried out of the room and looked for a secluded place where I could let the tears fall from my face in peace. I knew a closet was no good because things were constantly being taken out and used by the maids. I looked out one of the large windows at the beautiful garden.

"Perfect," I decided. Slipping out the window I ran through the beds of flowers to the very same place where I had met Mr. Fairday. He was gone now, and the path with graceful willow trees lay before me. I walked slowly down the path, taking refuge in the tranquil sounds of nature.

After a while, the path led me into a deeper part of the wood and I came upon a gazebo adorned with rose vines. Inside was a ring of gentle cushioned seats. I flopped down on the cushions as tears slipped off my eyelashes. "God, why did I have to mess up so bad? And why did she say such terrible things to me?!"

I was frustrated! If I *did* lose my job, how would Phillip go to school?!

"Please God," I prayed, "help me not get bitter toward Princess Vanessa. And please help Miss Primpette see that I am not as clumsy as I seem. In your precious name, Amen."

It wasn't a grand, elaborate prayer, but it was sincere and came from my heart. I opened my eyes to a brighter world and dried the tears from my eyes. Taking a deep breath I stood up resolutely. All of a sudden a familiar whistling tune floated through the air. My face brightened and I looked out of the gazebo expectantly. In a matter of seconds Mr. Frank Fairday came around the bend, holding a garden hose on his shoulder.

"Ah, Miss Noble, we meet again," he said smiling.

"Yes sir!" I said jumping out of the gazebo.

"Do I dare ask what you are doing out here again. Don't tell me the Queen didn't like her roses."

I laughed, "No, the Queen liked them very much! Actually, I am on a break."

"A break from work!" Mr. Fairday put his hands on his hips playfully. "Now wouldn't that be nice! How do you plan on spending it?"

I shrugged, "I'm not sure. Walk around I guess."

The elderly man's eyes twinkled, "How about visiting the Royal Stables? They have some amazing horses there."

"That would be great! Where is it?"

Mr. Fairday went on to say that the stables were on the west side of the gardens.

"You should find them quite easily. It just might happen that you'll meet a very nice young lad by the name of Carlos Santiago. He is one of the stable boys and a Christian. A very sturdy, hardworking lad he is, around your age too."

I thanked him very much and went on my way. "What interesting people God puts in my life," I exclaimed.

Chapter Four

Discoveries

$\mathcal{E}$ ver since I was a little girl in France I have adored horses! They are such gorgeous, majestic creatures!

Back in France, my grandmother had owned a horse named Poky (he was more like a tall, fat pig than a horse). Still, I loved that creature and drove poor Poky crazy by riding him nearly all the time!

I was very excited to see the horses in the Royal Stables – what a treat! The flowery gardens I was skipping through came to an end and a cobblestone road began. This road led me to a large building of stalls.

I could hear the whiny of some of the horses as they pranced in and out of the stables; either leading fancy carriages or going out for exercise.

I smiled with delightful anticipation while maneuvering in between all the commotion until I finally slipped inside!

A certain smell of wood, hay, horses, and manure filled my senses. I was quite impressed at how the whole place was kept with the utmost decency and cleanliness. In an attitude of high curiosity and amusement, I strolled through the building; looking anxiously into the stalls to see if there were any horses that caught my fancy.

Oh, were there ever! So many gorgeous horses I hardly knew which I liked best! They were strong, handsome, and distinguished animals! I couldn't help but stare in great admiration of their splendor!

Contrary to the commotion outside, the inside of the stables was quite mellow and calm. Warm sunlight filtered in through the tiny windows and gave a friendly glow to the pristine stables.

As I made my way to the farther end of the building, a very energetic whiny reached my ears. Turning a corner I beheld a large stall containing a breathtaking, pure, white, stallion!

My eyes became wide with wonder as I approached the spirited horse; I realized that this animal didn't have a spot or scar on his glossy white coat. His back was broad and strong, while his legs appeared sturdy and sure. His mane wasn't long, but not entirely too short. A golden chain hung about the stallion's graceful neck to finish off his kingly appearance.

The temptation to pet him was too strong to resist. Just one little pat wouldn't hurt, right? I was quite aware that this amazing creature probably wouldn't trust a total stranger. So, I quickly glanced around for some kind of food. Fortunately, I found a barrel of vegetables in one corner. Taking out a carrot, I leaned over the stall's gate and cautiously offered the carrot to the stallion. I was happily and surprisingly rewarded by having the horse not only eat the vegetable, but rub his soft nose on my face as well!

"Oh, you sweet thing," I exclaimed with a laugh. The stallion immediately began sniffing my dress for other treats. "I don't have any more," I replied looking into his large, brown eyes and patting his long face.

"Hey! Miss! What do you think you doing?!" a voice sharply called out.

Twirling around, I froze with sudden guilt. I was about to protest, but the sight of a lad coming towards me at a very fast pace caused me to hesitate. As he approached, I distinguished him to be about my age, with black, wavy hair, bronze skin, and attractive dark eyes that stared at me with reproof.

Getting quite nervous all of a sudden as he walked up to the stall, I began to explain in a fumbling voice, but he cut me short.

"Don't you know it is against the rules for anyone to enter the stalls without permission from the manager?" he stated with importance.

I wasn't willing to go through the ordeal of being made fun of again, so with an exasperated sigh I replied, "Forgive me! I had no intention of breaking any rules! I merely wanted to see and pet this beautiful animal. He's nearly flawless, and I've never seen such a wonderful horse."

The boy seemed surprised at my manner and studied me for a minute. "Well, for one thing it's a she, not a he. Secondly, perhaps I was a bit hasty. You appear to be new to the palace, and I shouldn't have expected a greenhorn to know the rules."

This was said in such a frank, kind tone that I couldn't help but smile. "Well," I replied, "I'm Jacqueline Noble, the greenhorn."

"And I'm Carlos Santiago, the stable boy," he said shaking my hand with a bright smile on his good looking face.

"Carlos Santiago," I repeated, "you're the boy Mr. Fairday said I should meet. He mentioned that you are a Christian."

"You bet I am! And you?"

"Likewise," I said making a curtsey.

He made a slight laugh, "You don't have to curtsey to me - I'm not the Queen."

"But it is proper decorum," I replied.

"That's a bunch of primpy, puffy nonsense made up by old ladies," he declared.

I tried to hide a smile, "Really?"

"Yeah! Just express yourself in a natural way," Carlos exclaimed with youthful enthusiasm.

I smiled, "And this is why I work in the palace, and you work in the stables."

Carlos grinned broadly at my answer, "You're alright Jacqueline – for a girl that is."

"Thanks, you're not so bad yourself."

After this introduction, Carlos and I got along quite well. I found that he was indeed a charming lad, though a bit rough around the edges. As he guided me through the rows of beautiful horses, Carlos finally asked why I had ventured into the Royal Stables.

So, I went on to explain what had happened that day and about the people I had met.

Carlos firmly agreed with me that Princess Vanessa was spoiled, and sympathized with my feelings towards her. However, he did confess that she was probably the prettiest creature he had ever seen.

I reluctantly agreed to this statement and tried to change the subject.

By this time, we had walked out of the Royal Stables and were venturing down the cobblestone road.

"Carlos, when did you accept Jesus?" I asked.

Spitting out the piece of straw he had been chewing, the boy related to me his unique tale.

It was quite a story!

Carlos was born and spent his early childhood in Spain. His father was a tough blacksmith, whose heart was sometimes as hard as the metals he worked with. Carlos's mother, however, was a very sweet, gentle soul. Neither of his parents knew the Lord.

One terrible day, a fire overtook their house and Carlos's father and mother died. Carlos was heartbroken and thought that no one in the world cared for him. Determined to make it on his own, at age twelve the young boy stowed away on a ship sailing for Lydonia.

The thirst for adventure and independence was enough to keep his mind occupied from the pain of the past. While sailing to Lydonia, Carlos met a kind Christian man named Bruce Steadfast (who is the pastor of Hope Congregation in Lyden). Pastor Steadfast shared the salvation message with the boy and Carlos accepted Jesus Christ into his heart.

Once the ship docked in Lydonia, Carlos looked for a job to support himself. However, Pastor Steadfast wouldn't hear of it and brought the lad under his roof. For a time, the reverend nurtured Carlos both spiritually and physically. When he came of age to work, Carlos decided to get his own job and take on the responsibilities of a young man.

"And now," Carlos concluded, "I work here. Sure it's not easy, but I get to live on the castle grounds as payment."

I blinked with surprise, "You live on the castle grounds. Where?"

"In one of the lofts at the Royal Stables. I can show you if you want, that is, after I get something to eat from the kitchen." He looked at me and smiled, "King Pasta will be glad I've brought a new visitor."

"King Pasta?!" I asked with a laugh.

"Si, he is the head chef for the palace. His real name is Ricky Pastaloni, from Italy, but I've nicknamed him King Pasta for short."

I was curious to meet this 'King Pasta' so I followed Carlos into the castle and down some stairs into a grand kitchen.

The whole place was abuzz with activity as cooks rushed around with ingredients and tasty dishes. Carlos took my hand and led me through the chaos to a huge stove where a very large, plump man, wearing a big fluffy hat, sipped a teaspoon of soup.

"Excellent!!" the man declared rubbing his hands together in rapturous pleasure. "This will certainly impress the Princess, though she has criticized everything I've made in the past!" and with a scowl the chef beat his fist into his palm.

"Excuse me! Sir?!" Carlos shouted above the noisy kitchen.

The chef turned around abruptly and was about to yell something back, but stopped when he saw Carlos. The chef smiled from under his thick, black mustache, "Ah my young rascal! You are hungry?"

"Si," Carlos replied, "and so is my friend, Jacqueline Noble."

"Ah! What a bella! Very nice to meet you!" Mr. Pasta exclaimed; his big hands wringing mine vigorously.

"Hi," I replied with a grin.

Carlos asked for a few apples and the kindly man readily gave them along with two sticks of sugar bread.

"Thank you sir!" I said gratefully.

"Don't eat them all at once lass, you'll get a stomach ache," the chef replied giving his big belly a fine slap.

I smiled and said I would do as he asked.

As Carlos and I ate our juicy apples, we left the kitchen and started walking back to the Royal Stables. Once there, Carlos led me to another section of the stables and up a ladder to a loft filled with soft hay. A stack of books lay in a corner beside a neat pile of clothes and blankets. A bed of hay was stationed underneath a bright skylight window which flooded the loft with natural light.

It may have been extremely simple but it looked warm and I was quite delighted with it!

"What do you want to be when you grow up?" I asked gazing at the stack of books. A Bible lay on the top.

Carlos sat down on a bed of hay and rested his back against the wooden wall. "I want to be a soldier in the Lydonian Military."

I rolled my eyes, "Why?!"

"Why not?"

"Well, it just seems that's what every man wants to do. My father died serving the Spanish Armada and my brother, Enrique, had the same urge and is now serving in the Lydonian Military. It's probably only a matter of time before he gets killed," I added under my breath.

Unfortunately, Carlos caught my mumbled remark.

"Don't talk like a sour puss," he stated.

I turned to see his flashing dark eyes.

"Enrique might come back a national hero!" he continued standing up. "Just imagine the exciting life he's living! Traveling the world! Combating with guns and swords! Fighting enemy forces to protect his home country!" he raised his hands in the air for a sign of victory. "You can't get much better than that. The adventure is endless!"

A smile broke out on my face as my imagination carried me far and wide, "Perhaps your right."

At that moment, we began to hear a voice from below calling, "Jacqueline! Jacqueline, are you here?"

I recognized the voice at once and answered at the top of the ladder, "I'm up here Lin!"

"What on earth are you doing up there?" she cried back.

"I was on a lunch break. Would you like to meet my new friend?"

"Sure, but she better come down to me because I'm in a hurry to return to work. The lunch break is over, and Miss Primpette wants you back on the job too."

"Who called me a she?!" Carlos asked joining me at the head of the ladder.

Lin blinked her eyes in surprise, "Oh! Sorry, I didn't know you were a. . .he."

"Carlos, this is Lin. Lin this is Carlos," I introduced.

"Nice to meet you," they both said at once. An awkward silence fell.

"Well," Lin said after a while, "let's get back to work."

I returned home that day very tired and worn out. The sun was sinking over the horizon in its entire splendor. I trudged along the green rolling hills leading to my little cottage. The gentle lilacs swayed softly in the warm evening breeze.

I opened the cottage door to the inviting scene of home. Phillip was playing energetically on the living room carpet while Mother tended the bubbling soup.

"Jackie!" Phillip exclaimed running towards me and hugging my legs tightly.

Mother turned around and gave me a bright smile. Wiping her hands on the apron, she came over and gave me a big hug and kiss, "Welcome home dear."

It really did feel good to be home.

"How was your first day?" Mother asked returning to the soup.

"Yeah, was the castle big?!" Phillip asked, his bright eyes sparkling.

I smiled, "Yes! The castle was *huge*."

"Was the work hard?" Mother asked as I hung up my brown bag.

"Yes, they expect perfection."

"Well, you can't blame them dear, remember, it is the home of the King and Queen."

"And Princess," I added with a sigh.

Mother looked at me, "And is Princess Vanessa nice?"

"Nice?!" I exclaimed with a sarcastic laugh. "Talk about torturous girls. Her own mother can't even stand her."

"That's pretty bad," Mother remarked with a half grin.

"And what's worse is that the Queen doesn't punish her!" I stated indignantly.

Mother shook her head, "Surely Jacqueline, you must have found something good at the palace."

My face softened as I told of Lin, Mr. Fairday, and Carlos. Phillip loved hearing my comical accounts of Edna, the maid, and the great King Pasta.

Mother encouraged me immensely and I felt so much better after family devotions.

"Family is so important," I thought to myself as I lay on my pillow; looking out the window at the blue twilight. I couldn't thank God enough for all the encouragement and love they gave me. With these pleasant thoughts, and the toil of the day's work pressing on my eyelids, I fell into a deep sleep.

In the morning I awoke with the early dawn and proceeded to start another day.

With kisses and hugs mom and Phillip sent me on my way. I walked down the road leading into the bustling, busy streets of Lyden.

Soon after I beheld the gates of the castle!

Following the example Miss Primpette had laid the day before, I turned left and went through the servants' entrance. Crossing the courtyard, I met Lin.

"I've been waiting for you to," she said as we embraced.

I smiled, "You didn't have to. I'm late as it is."

"Yeah, like five minutes late," Lin said with a laugh.

We walked arm in arm up the staircase into the east wing of the castle. Everything looked the same as yesterday, except for the fact that a huge group of maids, young and old, were gathering in the grand hall. All of them were chatting in low tones and looking up expectantly at the grand, white marble staircase.

"What is going on?" I murmured as Lin and I slowly advanced toward the unexpected gathering.

Lin shook her head in confusion, "I have no idea. Are they waiting for someone?"

"Looks like it," I remarked.

Lin and I joined the crowd quite unnoticed and made our way to the base of the staircase. This is where the gathering stopped, so we did not go farther. The whispering voices were all around us and it was nearly impossible not to overhear conversations.

My ears searched for a discussion that would enlighten my confusion. Sure enough, I discovered two old ladies talking about what today held in store.

"It's bound to be a fashionable affair," remarked one tight lipped maid.

"Aye," replied the other elderly maid, "I hear all of the rich lords and ladies in Lydonia are invited!"

"What a surprise! Do you mean to say they didn't invite me?" chuckled Tight Lip. "But I do not remember any occasion why this ball should take place. What is it for?"

The other short maid shrugged her skinny shoulders, "Who knows. Does it really matter? Princess Vanessa would have a ball every night if she could!"

"Ah, so the Princess instigated this festivity did she?" Tight Lip said with a raised eyebrow. "I'm guessing she plagued the poor Queen to have it. Ah, it's going to be busy day preparing for it."

"Quite so," replied Skinny Shoulders. Then, lowering her voice she exclaimed with a smile, "But I overheard a suspicion that this ball is to take place not just because the Princess wants it. The Queen is using it as an opportunity to select a future husband for her daughter."

"No!" exclaimed Tight Lip, her eyes shining with this juicy piece of gossip. "At such a young age, why she can't be more than fourteen!"

"Aye, but the Queen is going to arrange the matrimonial bond without the Princess knowing. Only when she comes of age will the marriage take place."

"Will the young man know he is committed to Her Highness?"

"I do not know all things!" exclaimed Skinny Shoulders with an annoyed air. "But, I pity him, whoever he is."

Both ladies chuckled heartily at this.

"So, we are assembled to prepare for the upcoming ball," I concluded to myself. I turned to relate this information to Lin, but before I could utter a sound, the crisp voice of Miss Primpette sounded in the grand hall.

"Thank you all for assembling here at my command," Miss Primpette began, "as you know Queen Tabitha is preparing a royal ball. I want everything done decently, orderly, and with perfection. I expect every one of you to do your duties with the utmost respect and loyalty to Her Majesty, Queen Tabitha."

An arousing cheer went up from the assembly and Miss Primpette continued, "Most of the Queen's maids will be partaking to help organize this event. It will take place in the Rose Ballroom and King Gilbert's elite selection of dinner guests will feast in the adjoining banquet hall. I will now split you all up into sections. Half of you will come with me and the other will be subject to the direction of this castle's wonderful Head Steward, Jacob Monroe."

A murmur of delight swept through the crowd and with a smile Miss Primpette added, "Mr. Monroe has been so kind as to lend a hand in this event."

Miss Primpette chose the right side to follow her into the banquet hall and the left half to meet Mr. Monroe in the Rose Ballroom. I was thankful there was a crowd to follow because I had no idea where the Rose Ballroom was – and neither did Lin.

Like a herd of sheep, the group of maids bustled out of the east wing and into the palace's central area. This place was even larger and grander than the Queen's hall – I was overwhelmed with the palace's beauty. The ceiling was so high I could barely distinguish the beautiful art painted on it.

The entire area was rather dome shaped with plenty of large, splendid windows to let in the sunlight. The romantic, swirling shapes on the marble floors made me want to twirl around and dance! Rich doors of all different styles appeared everywhere. Golden pillars stood majestically firm as they bore the weight of classical terraces. Lovely, long, twisting staircases presented themselves at every turn. The carpets were rich and soft, with all the elegance of royalty.

I was in raptures as my eyes went from one glorious thing to another. Unfortunately, this distracted my attention from the group of maids and I soon fell behind.

It was not long before I came to realize that the maids were nowhere in sight!

"Oh great!" I thought to myself. What was I supposed to do now?! I couldn't navigate through this place - that would take a lifetime!

To add to my misfortune, there was no one in sight to ask for help.

Looking frantically around for a human being, I happened to hear some voices coming from down a narrow hall to my right. My hope (and curiosity) urged me down the dim, red carpeted hall to see who these voices belonged to. With a quickening pace, I ventured farther down.

I passed opened and closed doors. I was hoping to see if my group was somewhere near here.

Suddenly, I collided harshly with a man coming out of a room!

The impact sent me reeling onto the floor. My rear end felt a pound of pain as it hit the ground. I winced and looked up to see who my adversary was.

The gentleman had obviously been hit pretty hard too, for he uttered a groan and his hand felt his stomach. "You are one sturdy miss! Watch where you're going next time!"

I was fully prepared to shoot back an unladylike comment; however, my eyes were too busy staring at the dashing man before me. If his figure had been less attractive or his face slightly less handsome, I might have had the courage to say something rash – but I could not. Instead, I lamely replied, "I guess I'm the one who's supposed to apologize then?"

"No, I was reckless - it was my fault altogether," the man replied gallantly as he helped me to my feet. He smiled pleasantly and bowed slightly, "Who is it that I owe my apologies?"

"Jacqueline Noble," I replied quietly while my cheeks blushed in the dim light. Granted, I was slipping into a silly and naïve state of mind; but what is a girl supposed to do when faced with such a man?

"A very fine name for a very fine young lady," he remarked.

"And you are?" I asked.

"Jacob Monroe," he answered offering his hand.

"Thank goodness!" I exclaimed so suddenly that he started. "I've been looking for the group of maids that were to meet in the Rose Ballroom. I am one of them under your command."

"Well, that is fortunate! I shall be very pleased to have such a pretty and sturdy young girl working for me," he declared with an affirming nod. "Now, if you will follow me I will lead you to the Rose Ballroom myself."

I eagerly accepted Mr. Monroe's offer.

We walked out of the hallway and into a doorway on the far end of the palace's central area. Two corridors wound around either side of the Rose Ballroom and joined together at an entrance to a beautiful garden.

When we entered the ballroom my eyes became wide with awestruck delight! I wouldn't have been surprised to see Cinderella sweep by, because this ballroom was truly enchanting.

The floor was soft pink in color with rose designs swirling all over it. Graceful tapestries hung on the walls and roses strung with pearls decorated the doorways. Several arched openings in the wall allowed passage to the two corridors that surrounded this elegant area.

"Oh Mr. Monroe, this is wonderful!" I exclaimed with pleasure. "Does the castle have more than one ballroom?"

"Yes," he replied, "it has three in fact: the Rose, the Crystal, and the Garden Ballroom. But between you and me, this is my favorite."

As we neared the chatting group of maids, several of them gave my tall escort dreamy glances and pretty smiles. Obviously Mr. Monroe's pleasing manners and appearance were not unknown.

Some ladies cast me looks of envy as he glided me to the front of the line.

I did not allow myself time to feel either pride or embarrassment; for my focus was soon preoccupied with finding Lin.

Mr. Monroe backed out so he could survey his company and then address them.

Before he began to speak, I felt a nudge at my elbow and someone squeeze in between me and another maid.

"Hello," Lin said as she straightened up beside me.

"Hi," I replied with a smile.

"What happened to you?"

"I became distracted with the loveliness of the palace and lost sight of you. Sorry."

"No need to apologize," Lin remarked with a grin. "Where did you meet 'Prince Charming'? Was he part of your unfortunate distraction?"

I gave my friend a sharp look and tried to turn her sensible again. "Don't be absurd. Mr. Monroe was merely being a gentleman in showing me the way back."

Lin just smiled and shrugged as everyone turned their attention to the Head Steward.

We were all assigned specific duties and given the equipment to perform them. Lin and I were to scrub the ballroom floor, clean the tapestries, put fresh roses to cover the doorways and I could go on with the list.

It was work - *hard* work. Morning till noon we bent our backs in labor for the upcoming festival. To add to the pleasantries, it was very hot outside and no different inside. Sweat trickled down my forehead as my hands scrubbed hard to polish the ballroom floor.

"Gracious," I remarked to Lin, "if I keep this up, I'll have more muscles than a military general."

Lin smiled and then began to laugh. . .and laugh. . .and laugh.

"It wasn't *that* funny," I remarked with a grin.

"Yes it is! Just imagine big hunks of muscles on your neck, arms and legs! You look ridiculous!"

I just stared at her – trying to see how it was so hilarious.

"Sorry," she said trying to calm down. "I guess I'm dying for some humor."

"Oh you're dying all right," I said with a laugh.

She threw her wet sponge on my face and I repaid it by sitting my soapy mop on her head. We both laughed and threw a few wet, sloppy things at each other before Miss Primpette came bustling toward us commanding, "Stop! Stop! Ladies! Control yourselves!"

Just as she said this, the lady slipped on a puddle of water and fell into her many layers of skirts! Poof!

That was about the only fun Lin and I had until the lunch break. When that time came, both of us ran to one of the fountains in the royal gardens and splashed cool water all over our faces. Sweet relief! It felt *so* good.

After that we debated on what to do. We wanted to amuse ourselves for a while. I suggested we go see Carlos and get a bite to eat at 'King Pasta's' kitchen. This was agreed upon and so we made our way over to the Royal Stables.

The day was very bright - and hot. But the shade of trees and the occasional blow of wind soothed the atmosphere.

"Those poor horses having to stay in hot confined stalls. It must be unbearable!" I exclaimed as Lin and I neared the Royal Stables.

"I bet it's not as horrible as you make it out to be. We've been working all day and the horses merely rest in the safe shade of the stables. They're probably better off then you think," Lin reassured as we climbed up the ladder that led to Carlos's loft.

Well, the stalls might have been cool, but Carlos's loft wasn't. No sir, it was steaming! It was hard to believe Carlos was comfortable living here under such weather.

"Poor boy," I muttered.

Lin wiped her forehead, "It's sure hot up here. Did you say he *lives* here?"

"Yep. He's very. . ."

"Proud of it!" a voice behind us exclaimed. Carlos came up the ladder; his face was bright and happy. However, I noticed his tan skin had a dewy appearance and his wavy black hair was rather damp from sweat.

"This place is too hot for you. What if you catch a fever?" Lin declared; hands on her hips.

Carlos rolled his eyes and replied, "Don't get all nervous. I've been working all day in the hot sun that's why I'm sweaty - not because the loft is warm."

"All the same Carlos, you can't be content having to sit in this frying pan," I remarked.

A twinkle of delight flashed in the boy's dark eyes as he evasively replied, "I have my ways of staying cool. I certainly don't stay here all day!"

"What do you do?" Lin stated. I could tell she didn't quite like Carlos's frank, playful attitude.

"Wouldn't you like to know," the boy shot back.

For a moment the stares of both my friends rose to a higher temperature than the room. Trying to simmer down the atmosphere, I walked in-between them and suggested, "So, whose hungry? Why don't we all go down to the kitchen and grab some food?"

Both of them really liked this idea so, in a state of peace, we headed towards the palace.

Chapter Five

A Good Sign

*I*f I mentioned that the royal kitchen is busy place, it is even crazier when preparing for a ball! All kinds of extravagant foods are being made with the greatest care and artistic taste. Cakes were in abundance as well as roast chicken and caviar.

Despite the bustling activity, Lin, Carlos and I reached Chef Pastaloni with little difficulty. However, as we approached 'King Pasta' it became evident that he was not in a good mood – in fact, he was in a fit of rage!

We watched in silence as he marched through the kitchen; fists clenched and declaring, "Nobody refuses Chef Pastaloni's food! Never, never!"

"What's wrong sir?" Carlos asked.

"Ah my boy, you will not believe what I have been through. Rejection to one's food is hard to bear, but when Princess Vanessa does it the torture is criminal! She turned down my soup and then threw it at me in front of all the cooks!"

Lin looked amused and turned her face to conceal a smile.

I knew better than to laugh at the fiery chef's misfortunes and nudged Lin to control herself.

Carlos put his arm around the heavy set man and said soothingly, "It is not that bad sir. Everyone is disgraced by the Princess now and then."

"She shall never disgrace me again! Of that I will make certain!" and with flaming eyes, 'King Pasta' retreated into another part of the kitchen.

All of us were frozen in one place for a few minutes until Carlos turned around and said, "Don't worry he'll get over it."

Lin smiled, "Does he usually act in this blustering way?"

Carlos shrugged as he rummaged through a fruit basket, "No. But he is very sensitive about his food. I certainly don't blame him for being upset! Princess Vanessa's reckless temper gets on everyone's nerves at some point." He tossed me a soft peach and gave Lin an orange.

We made our way out of the kitchen and into a very vast, green part of the castle grounds. Carlos explained that these hills were used for the horses' daily exercise routines.

Thankfully, the weather was cooling down immensely as clouds started to fill the sky. All of us sat down on a lush sloping hill to eat our fruit.

After a while I suggested we lie on our backs and make out cloud shapes.

Everyone liked the idea! So, the three of us lay down and came up with the most interesting objects for the passing clouds. It was a lot of fun - the three of us laughing, talking, and dreaming.

"So Lin, are you going to go to church with Jacqueline?" Carlos asked.

"I don't know. I'm thinking about it."

"You really should. I go there too and it would be so much fun if we all went."

Lin shrugged.

I didn't want to pressure Lin to come. If she really wanted to, then she would. "If you do decide to go Lin, my family and I would be happy to take you."

"Thank you," she replied quietly. Lin didn't say anything for a while and I tried to busy my mind with the beautiful environment.

Suddenly Lin said, "One of the reasons I'm nervous to attend church is that I don't have a great past with religion. My family back in China was very strict in their native religion. So much that when they found out my father had bore a child unmarried, they abandoned him forever. My father and I had to flee our country because we didn't want to have to bear the shame of cruel rejection all our lives." Lin's voice quivered as she gave us a glimpse of the pain she had suffered.

"Well," I began gently, "at least you live here now – your father must be happy about that."

Lin gave a slight, sarcastic smile, "Sure."

Carlos and I were silent. I couldn't find the right words to say so I put my arm around my friend and squeezed her tight. Lin squeezed back and rested her head on my shoulder.

"Oh God," I prayed, "save Lin' soul and show here how much you love her!"

Carlos comforted Lin the best he could by sharing his testimony of how he had lost everything, when Jesus entered his life and turned him around!

Lin paid close attention and seemed very interested in everything the boy said.

"Perhaps I will come to church. But I don't think my father will so. . ."

"I can take you!" I volunteered cheerfully.

"I guess if you take me it will be alright," Lin decided.

Carlos slapped his knee in enthusiastic victory, "Awesome!"

And that is the day that three kids became very good friends.

The next morning was Sunday and the entire Noble family was busy getting dressed in their best. Not that we had a lot of fancy clothes to wear, but as Mother always says, 'If your going to church to worship Jesus, dress like your going to meet the King'.

So with this in mind, I brushed my soft ringlets of hair into a bun and put on the pearl necklace my father had given to me before his ship sunk. My head always fills with memories when this luminous piece of jewelry graces my neck. My father was one of the greatest Christians I will ever know. I miss him dearly. Thinking of him made me remember Lin and her father. Such silent agony that family must be carrying inside their heavy souls! It brought tears to my eyes.

Mother's voice brought me to reality and I straightened my blue muslin dress, placed a mob cap on my head, and hurried downstairs.

Phillip was stiff and starch in his Sunday outfit and it was quite comical observing how he tried to constrain his energetic impulses. His self-control didn't last. Soon he was whooping and running all around to the dismay of Mother and me.

"Well, what can you expect of a five year old?" Mother sighed as she straightened her lovely hat in the mirror. "Now, if we are going to walk Lin to church we better get going."

This was enough motivation for me to hurry up and drag Phillip outside. The morning air was crisp and cool, for there had been a very heavy rainstorm last night. It took all of my womanly powers to prevent Phillip from playing in the mud. Why boys find pleasure in such things I cannot comprehend!

I was grateful when Mother came out and we started down the road leading to the town of Lyden. Hope

Congregation is on the far, west side of the town centered on a nice little acre of lush green grass. The Dogwood Hills are directly behind the church and are particularly beautiful during this season of the year. Lin would really like them, of that I was sure.

We entered Lyden and made our way down the main street to the Spice Shop. This is the place Lin's father owns; he works downstairs and upstairs is where the Chang family lives. The shop windows were dark and the door was locked.

"Strange," Mother murmured as she knocked on the door.

I became a little anxious. What if Lin had changed her mind? Perhaps Mr. Chang did not approve. I bit my lip as mother knocked a second time.

Presently footsteps were heard inside and a light came on. The door was unlocked and an oriental man of about thirty seven stood before us. His dark brown eyes spoke of an intelligent and learned mind while his firm jaw revealed a decided character. I could tell he was scanning me and my family to see if he could trust us.

"Well, at least Lin has a protective father," I said to myself.

"You must be Mrs. Noble," he said extending his hand cordially.

"Yes, it is a great pleasure to meet you Mr. Chang. Is Lin coming with us?" Mother asked sweetly.

Mr. Chang nodded in his solemn way and turned behind him, beckoning Lin to come.

Lin stepped into the doorway with a smile on her face. She had on a beautiful Chinese silk dress. I smiled back warmly.

"I'm so glad you are allowing Lin to join us. Jacqueline was so excited as well as Phillip. Weren't you my dears?"

I nodded at Mother with enthusiasm. My eyes glanced down at Phillip; unfortunately my little brother was too intimidated by Mr. Chang to do anything but stare. I nudged him and he blinked a couple of times and then mechanically smiled.

The Dogwood Hills were in full bloom and gave such a beautiful background for Hope Congregation that it seemed almost fairylike. Lin's eyes became bright with delight when she saw all of the trees and their glorious white flowers.

"It's like heaven," she murmured.

"Something like it," I replied smiling.

The attendants of Hope Congregation were already filling the seats when we entered. It was a very pretty, quaint sort of building that was large enough to hold the growing congregation. Now that I knew Carlos and Mr. Fairday also attended this church, my eyes scanned the pews for a glimpse of them. My efforts were rewarded for among the front pews sat the stable boy and the gardener. Both of them were chatting away with Pastor Steadfast's family.

The pastor's family was a good-humored bunch including Pastor Bruce and Mrs. Ellen Steadfast and their twin children who were a year older than me. Their names were Roger and Rose.

I pointed them out to Lin and asked Mother if our family could sit with them. Mother happily agreed and so we made our way over to the group.

Mr. Fairday immediately got up and shook all of our hands in such a warm, hearty way that I felt he could have been my grandfather. Carlos was very happy to see us but reluctant to leave his conversation with the gentle, sweet pastor's daughter. Mrs. Steadfast gave smiles and hugs all around and was soon engaged in a conversation with Mother.

Mr. Fairday turned to us with a smile, "It is so good to see you three here. I do believe it was the Lord's leading that we met each other at the castle."

"You didn't meet me!" Phillip remarked with his usual enthusiasm.

"Quite right young man," Mr. Fairday exclaimed as he bent down to my younger brother's level. "My name is Mr. Frank Fairday. What is yours?"

"Phillip Estaban Noble!" he replied jumping up and down. I was surprised my brother could articulate such a name.

I could see Mr. Fairday was very pleased. The elderly man enjoyed the little boy's energy immensely (probably because he didn't have any).

So while Phillip and Mr. Fairday got better acquainted, Lin and I busied ourselves by being introduced to the Steadfast twins. I had a very distant acquaintance with the twins and was eager to know them more.

Carlos was very excited for us to meet them because they had been his first Christian friends while Pastor Steadfast had taken care of him.

"Jacqueline, Lin, this is Rose and Roger," Carlos introduced.

The modest girl curtseyed and smiled at us. I did not know what to make of her at first. Rose was so cordial and pleasant that I didn't have much insight into her real character at all. She was very polite and unassuming with innocent brown eyes. Her features consisted of wavy auburn hair, delicate fair skin and a dimple on her right cheek that showed every time she smiled. I found her to be very sincere and charming!

Her brother on the other hand was a different story. Roger was simply impossible to discern. His actions and words were sometimes so vague and unnoticeable that you wondered if he was too shy or proud to share his opinions at all. He was not much different in features than his twin sister except that he was not a girl. He had intelligent brown eyes, wavy auburn hair and medium skin tone. When Carlos introduced him to us, Roger bowed slightly and smiled timidly.

"Poor boy," I thought, "he really is a shy thing." But it's the quiet ones you have to watch out for, because they absorb and watch everything you do.

Lin was very civil to the twins but I could see nothing more than that. My friend seemed kind of tense and anxious. Trying to loosen her nerves I tried leading her and Rose in a conversation.

"So Rose, Carlos tells me you like silk," I began.

She nodded, "Yes, I do."

"Well, Lin's father used to make silk in China."

"Really? How interesting! Do you have a favorite color?" Rose asked.

Lin recognized my efforts for socialization and gratefully complied, "Well, I do adore purple silk."

"How nice! White is my silk color. I would like pink but Mother says that such a color does not look good with my red hair. I think purple silk would suit you very well."

I was happy with my success and sat down quite contented. Nearly everyone in the church had taken their seats by now and waited for the choir to start singing.

As I turned my head Carlos caught my eye. He gave me an approving nod and cocked his head in the direction of Lin and Rose. Both girls were chatting away like old friends.

I smiled back and turned my attention to the pulpit. A group of church members stood in their assigned places and began to sing a hymn. All the talking amongst the congregation stopped and everyone stood; joining the singers in their praise to God.

I love worshipping Christ Jesus with the entire body of believers! There's just something heavenly about hearing Christians lifting their voices in thankfulness to the Lord.

When the singing had ended, everyone sat down and Pastor Bruce Steadfast walked up to the pulpit. He was a tall man with a good-looking face, light brown hair and piercing hazel eyes. "Brothers and sisters in the Lord, welcome!" he greeted extending his arms to the congregation. With that, the virtuous Reverend shared a wonderful sermon to the people's open hearts.

He talked about being aware of sin and the destruction it can do to our lives. The primary scripture verse was Matthew 7:15 "Watch out for false prophets. They come to you in sheep's clothing, but inwardly they are ferocious wolves."

Pastor Steadfast taught that very often sinful people and deeds don't look dangerous or even bad. They seem harmless and perhaps good, but if peoples' motives are not aligned with the word of God, their deeds are just as wicked as 'obvious' sins. He also reminded the congregation to be cautious of false prophets; who are people that appear good but are inwardly selfish, ferocious wolves.

"God commands us to be wise as serpents and harmless as doves. Some people get one side of the coin right but forget the other entirely. A person can be as wise as a serpent but venomous in words and deeds. And yet, a person can be harmless as a dove but flimsy in descision and wisdom. So, when faced with a false prophet or a deceptive person, we must use discretion which is a combination of wisdom and sensitivity. We can only be responsible for ourselves. But when we see sin in our own lives we *must* repent and ask God to help us change the way we act."

My eyes glanced over at Lin who sat beside me. I was surprised and pleased to find she was paying close attention to the sermon.

Pastor Steadfast ended by saying that no one can accomplish what he had been talking about this morning unless that person became born again. Accepting Jesus into one's heart was the greatest and best thing they could ever do.

He talked about how unending God's love was for us and beckoned anyone who wished to commit his life to Jesus to come forward. A couple of people left their seats and slowly came down the aisle. A rapturous applaud went up from the people, congratulating these new believers on their momentous decision.

Did Lin go down to the altar? Sadly, no.

She did applaud when the other people went down, but she did not follow them.

I admit I was disappointed. My mind knew she probably wouldn't go down her first time hearing a sermon, but my heart had hoped. But as Mother told me, 'It's the Holy Spirit that must lead a person to salvation, not necessarily you.'

When the service ended and our family said goodbye to the Steadfasts, Mr. Fairday, and Carlos, we headed out the doors and back home.

The sun was so bright and the air so refreshing that my spirits became lighter. The beautiful trees swayed easily in the breeze while the chirping of a bird could be heard as it fluttered through the air. A smile split my face and I purposed within myself to think only of cheerful things.

"So Lin, how did you like the sermon?" Mother asked.

"It was very. . .interesting. Thank you for taking me Mrs. Noble."

"Anytime dear. We would love it if you joined us next week," Mother invited.

Lin nodded enthusiastically, which I thought was a good sign.

Chapter Six

The Ballroom Night

*T*he next day was spent in continuous preparation for the evening ball. Now that the cleaning was done, decorating the Rose Ballroom had begun! This part was much more pleasant then the first. Hanging up floral tassels and lighting candles on chandeliers is quite more enjoyable than scrubbing floors.

Mr. Monroe directed us in such a kind, orderly way that it was a grand pleasure to work under him. Miss Primpette stuck her head in every now and then to see how things were operating (and to sneak a glance at our director) and was pleased to find the ballroom growing more and more splendid. It was indeed a beautiful sight to behold!

Tables of delicious food stood in one corner of the elegant area while an orchestra was to be seated near the right of the garden door. Magnificent, gold chandeliers flooded the romantic dance floor with warm light and rose vines strung with pearls graced the arched doorways.

Lin and I viewed the scene with rapturous pleasure!

"Truly, I have never seen such a beautiful place!" Lin murmured.

"It's even lovelier because we're the ones who worked on it," I remarked with a smile.

"Correct," Lin replied, "and it is such a pity that we won't even be able to attend the ball!"

"I don't know about that."

Lin turned to me, "What do you mean?"

"Well, I asked Mother last night if I could watch the ball take place from one of these openings." I pointed to the arched entranceways leading to a corridor that encircled the ballroom.

"The corridor is used by servants to help with the ball without disturbing the guests'. Mother agreed that I could come and observe the rich party if someone was with me." I turned to Lin.

A look of disappointment crossed my friends face. "I know my father will not consent to such a plan. He wants me home very early so I can help with the spices."

My countenance fell. Oh how I wanted to see the ball! All of my visions of delight vanished from my mind.

"But," Lin continued, "I can stay with you for the beginning of the ball. Perhaps Carlos can accompany you with the rest."

"That's a good idea!" I said with renewed energy. "I'll ask Carlos."

"Are you crazy?!" Carlos cried when I asked the favor.

We were standing in his loft home.

"Please Carlos, I need someone with me. Lin can't stay so my only other option is you."

"To attend a ball!" the boy repeated as if the idea was completely beyond his ability and comprehension.

"Well it's not like I'm asking you to dance at the ball!"

"Good! Because I can't dance either!" he answered while dropping down on a bale of hay.

I smiled and rolled my eyes, "You are such a typical boy. I'm just asking if you could watch the event with me, nothing more."

Carlos looked up with skeptical eyes, "That's it. No catch?

"No catch."

The stable boy gave a sigh and ran his hand through his wavy black hair, "Okay, fine."

"Well I'm so glad you can accompany me on such an impossible feat," I replied with a grin.

"Just don't tell any of the stable guys - they'll laugh me to my grave if you do!" Carlos warned.

I laughed and shook my head, "I wouldn't dream of it."

So, with this settled I went about my chores as happy as a lark.

When evening came I made a short trip home to get the shawl Mr. Dilamari had given me. I wanted to wear the lovely piece of clothing as I witnessed the enchanting night at the Rose Ballroom.

"Be sure to stay inside if it gets chilly," Mother reminded.

"Yes Mother."

"And make sure nothing spills on your dress."

"I will."

"Stay with Carlos or Lin the whole time."

"You got it."

"And Jacqueline. . ."

"Yes?"

"Don't lose the shawl," Mother said gently.

"I won't. I love you!" I said heading out the cottage door.

"Jackie!" Phillip called before I left.

"What?"

"Bring me back some cake pleeeease!"

I smiled, "I'll try. Goodbye!"

And with that, I was off!

Fireflies were beginning to glow in the evening dusk as I walked through the grassy hills. A breeze blew a few wisps of loose hair from my styled bun and rustled the gentle fabric of my treasured shawl. Yes, it was going to be a beautiful night!

I skipped down the red dirt road leading to the lighted buildings of Lyden. Suddenly I heard hooves pounding and horses whinnying behind me.

I turned around just in time to avoid being run over by the wheels of a very fancy carriage. I looked on with contempt as the stylish coachman whipped the white stallions; attempting to quicken their pace towards their destination. The occupants of such a piece of luxury must be very wealthy.

"They're probably going to the ball," I mused within myself.

Knowing that more carriages were bound to come down the same road I walked faster; keeping to the side of the highway.

Several aristocratic carriages past me and I knew the ball would start soon. With renewed energy I flew through the town and made my way to the palace – I could not be late!

I arrived out of breath at the castle's golden gates. I had always seen the gates closed so it was quite new to view them wide open with countless regal carriages gliding through the main entrance. Lords, Ladies, Dukes, Duchesses, Governors and all their families stepped out of elegant coaches and displayed their fashionable splendor.

I stood mesmerized for a moment until one of the guards caught my attention and ordered me to move along.

I hurried into the servant's quarters and up to the castle's east wing. The grand hall was quiet and grave as a tomb; however, my eyes caught a glimmer of light shining from one of the doors on the second floor. Faintly, I heard voices.

Slowly I made my way up the white marble staircase.

Queen Tabitha's bedroom and dress room lights were shining brightly as the Ladies in Waiting pampered Her Highness. The dressing room door was cracked open so I cautiously crept up to it and peeked inside.

My eye beheld the Queen sitting on a plush pink chair in front of a large mirror; powdering her face and reddening her lips and cheeks. She wore a very elegant white wig that was adorned with diamonds and a few luscious flowers. An emerald gown with white lace graced Her Majesty's fine figure. The Ladies in Waiting were drowning the Queen with flattery and exaggerated shrieks of delight!

I watched as Kelsey and Charlotte (the two Ladies in Waiting) graciously hand their mistress sparkling jewelry.

"You look fantastic my Queen!" Charlotte gushed as she placed a pearl necklace around the lady's neck.

The Queen made no comment but continued to study her complexion in the mirror.

"Here you are madam," Kelsey said as she reverently handed Her Majesty two emerald earrings.

"Thank you ladies," the Queen replied in a tone that betrayed her annoyance. "Now, please don't feel obligated to accompany me through the entire evening. I give you leave to go enjoy yourselves."

The two teenage girls' eyes sparkled.

"Oh! That would be delightful Your Highness!" Kelsey said with a little jump and a clap of her hands.

"Do you think there will be many young men there my Queen?" Charlotte asked.

Queen Tabitha smiled, "Oh yes, I am counting on it."

The two Ladies in Waiting gave a girlish giggle.

"Now then, off you go," the Queen said with a graceful wave of her hand.

And so the two girls exited the room through another door, giggling and whispering excitedly the whole time.

I thought their behavior was some of the most ridiculous I had ever seen! Getting all hyped up because of the chance to see some eligible men. "What a waste of energy! I will never be so light headed," I said to myself with a firm nod. I was beginning to back away from the door when I felt a hand clasp my shoulder.

"Spying are we?" a familiar voice snapped.

I turned around and nearly bumped my head on the waist of. . .Miss Primpette!

I stared wide eyed at the tall imposing figure of the Maid Supervisor. "No Miss Primpette! I wouldn't spy, I was just. . ."

"Just what?" the lady asked bending down so her sharp, narrow eyes could meet mine directly.

I gulped hard. For the moment my voice left me and I had no idea how to respond to the lady's scary, reproving look.

Just as I was about to apologize, the door swung open and Queen Tabitha herself stepped out.

"Miss Primpette! What are you doing here? Did you want me?" Her Majesty asked.

Miss Primpette seemed a bit ruffled that she had been discovered and gave a very vague reply.

"And what is going on with this sweet girl?" Her Majesty asked looking at me with a kind smile.

"Ah, this is one of your maids my Queen - and I caught her peeking through the door!" Miss Primpette said triumphantly.

"Forgive me Your Majesty, I am terribly sorry! I didn't mean to intrude on your privacy," I said with pleading eyes.

With her usual warm smile, Queen Tabitha forgave me completely and dismissed me only with a warning. But I knew Miss Primpette was offended that the Queen hadn't punished me to the full extent (a feeling I could relate to). Still, I was grateful for my escape!

I nearly ran the whole way to the Rose Ballroom, all the while looking around for Lin. I came to the ballroom entrance and stopped to marvel at the extravagance and glory of the whole scene.

The blissful moment was cut short for I soon became aware that Lin was running up to me from down the corridor.

"There you are!" I exclaimed.

"I've been waiting for you. Come on! Let's watch the party from the corridor to the right, there's a good view of the orchestra and the dance floor."

I rushed along with Lin as she led me down the corridor to an arched opening that commanded a large view of the Rose Ballroom.

"This is a perfect place! I can see nearly everyone here!" I remarked. We both stood there for a few minutes, watching the beautiful event take place.

"Isn't it simply glorious," Lin said dreamily.

I nodded with the same faraway expression, "Yeah, I wish I could put on a flowing gown and glide across the dance floor."

"I would too, except that the ladies seem so stiff when they dance," Lin commented.

I blinked and tried to see what Lin meant. "Your right! They do look rather awkward and stiff! How silly! Couldn't they just move their body to the motion of the music?"

My friend shrugged, "It's not the fashion I suppose. It's etiquette to dance that way."

I sniffed, "Etiquette indeed!"

So we both stood there, observing all that happened during the beginning of the ball. Some of the people were beautiful, ugly, interesting, dull, and so forth. So, we decided to name some of them; one was Grumpy, another Cinderella, then Moose Man, Crow Nose, Blue Eyes – well - you get the idea. It was great fun!

After a while, Charlotte and Kelsey came near our spot. Both of them were so busy chatting they didn't even notice Lin and me. Most of their conversation consisted of. . .men. I felt ready to puke. Was there anything else in the world they could talk about!

"Well, which do you think the Queen will set Princess Vanessa up with?" Kelsey asked Charlotte.

"Of course Her Majesty will pick the two handsomest young men in the room," Charlotte replied with an air of importance.

"And who do you think they are?" Kelsey prodded with eager eyes.

"Why Dennis Arlow and Charlie Worthington of course."

"Yes I quite agree! It's interesting to watch how amused and flattered the young gentlemen are with Princess Vanessa's flirtation! Hopefully they recognize how absurd she is and pay greater attention to more deserving ladies – like us!" Kelsey remarked with a smiling sigh.

"Unfortunately, such a hope is rather dim," Charlotte replied.

A moment of rare silence passed between the two Ladies in Waiting.

I gave a little sigh of satisfaction and Lin stifled a giggle. She knew that I considered such talk boring and silly. The Ladies in Waiting did not let me rest long and once again started jabbering.

"I really do think Dennis Arlow is the most charming and good looking young man in the world," Charlotte sighed dreamily.

Kelsey gave an indignant laugh, "Really, I cannot agree with that. Charlie Worthington is far more handsome. As to charming, the young lord is known for being the definition of such a word. You just like Dennis better because he winked at you."

And with that new argument, the two girls went away.

I breathed another sigh of relief and rolled my eyes, "Thank goodness their gone!"

Lin laughed and then affecting a serious tone said, "Which do you like best Jacqueline, Sir Arlow, or Lord Worthington?"

I gave Lin a look. My friend's eyes glistened with merry mischief.

I shrugged in response, "All I will say is that Kelsey has better judgment than Charlotte."

Lin imitated Kelsey's voice, "I quite agree with you."

We both burst out laughing.

Our attention refocused on the ballroom just as King Gilbert and Queen Tabitha were announced.

Everyone stood at attention as the royal couple came through the main entranceway. A beautiful lute played as the perfect pair took their regal seats at the head of the Rose Ballroom. Princess Vanessa had already taken her seat on the left side of the King.

Everyone raised their glasses to the royal family and in one accord said, "King Gilbert, may you live long in strength, wisdom and glory! Queen Tabitha, may your grace and honor be known throughout the earth! Princess Vanessa, may your beauty bloom to everlasting! Long live the royal family of Lydonia!"

"And may our fair country always be blessed," King Gilbert replied.

All cheered to this and the party resumed its course.

I had always been interested to see King Gilbert – after all, he was the King!

Now that I had met his family, I wanted to see what type of man he was. He was about six foot, with a clean shaven face, robust build, and wise, penetrating eyes; an air about him spoke plainly that he was large and in charge. His disposition and mind appeared much more mature than his wife and daughter's. I did feel sorry for him – having to bear such a family. However, his family's present state is partly his fault. King Gilbert is often so occupied with Lydonia's affairs that he hardly spends time with the Queen and Princess - a very sad thing. Aside from this, His Majesty did seem very kind and noble.

After I had satisfied my curiosity with the King, several lively dances started playing and the room was filled with a sweet, classic melody.

It was so enjoyable! I have always had a love for music, but the hardest time learning to play it! Lin on the other hand, mentioned that she could play the harp.

"How did you learn to play the harp?!" I asked in astonishment.

"Years ago, when my father and I moved to Lydonia, the lady who taught me the language also introduced me to the harp. I learned how to play then, but I'm not so sure I can do the same now."

"Oh you must!" I said earnestly. I racked my brain trying to think of someone I knew who owned a harp. "Rose Steadfast! She owns a harp I believe. I don't think she would mind you using it, both of you hit it off so well at church."

"Thanks to you," Lin replied smiling.

Just as she said this the dance ended and the music died down. Lin looked up at a clock on the wall of the ballroom.

"I have to go, father will be worried about me," she informed. We both hugged tightly and said goodbye. Lin promised that Carlos would be here soon.

While waiting for Carlos to arrive, I decided to go around the Rose Ballroom using the passage of the two corridors winding around the area. It was quite interesting to see the event and people from different angles. I was not surprised to find that Princess Vanessa was indeed a big flirt. Queen Tabitha approached several young men and began friendly conversations with them (no doubt testing to see if they would be a good match for her daughter).

Gentleman talked of politics, war, and hunting, while the ladies fluttered their fans chatting about fashion, family, and gossip.

I was just returning to the right side of the corridor when I saw Carlos coming in my direction.

"There you are," I said, "I was wondering if you had the guts to keep up your promise."

He made a face, "Very funny. Don't think I'm the only guy who doesn't like this girly stuff."

"Girly stuff! Even guys go to balls. Besides, it *is* very intriguing - you actually might enjoy watching the people act the way they do."

Carlos raised a skeptical eyebrow but joined me at the doorway.

It so happened he did find it enjoyable. We made more names for the people and had a good time listening to the music and watching the graceful dances.

"It would be more fun if we were actually *in* the party," Carlos remarked after a while.

"Yeah, but beggars can't be choosers," I stated. I put my hand on my shoulder and a sudden wash of anxiety overcame me. "Where was it?" I thought frantically. My other hand felt my back and then my eyes scanned the floor. It was gone!

"What's wrong?" Carlos asked after watching me spin around a few times.

"I lost it! Mother's going to kill me!"

"Lost what?"

"A beautiful shawl I had that was a present from Mr. Dilamari. Mother instructed me to *not* lose it. What do ya know? I lost it!" I unconsciously ran my hand through my hair and ruined the fancy bun. "Ah! My bun! Oh this is just great."

"Calm down," Carlos said picking up my hairpins. "We'll look around okay, no problem. Your hair looks just as good down as up."

"You don't wear your hair down for special occasions – especially balls!"

"For goodness sake! You girls are so darn picky!" Carlos exclaimed thrusting the hairpins into my hand.

I smiled. It was fun getting on Carlos' nerves and the enjoyment relaxed me for a bit. To find the shawl, we decided that the best thing to do was check the two corridors I had recently walked through.

The evening dusk had transformed into night which left hardly any light in the dark halls of the castle except for the flickering candles. The dimly lit left corridor was even darker than I had expected. The sound of our shoes was muffled by the long red carpet as candlelight cast our wavering shadows upon the palace walls.

Carlos crouched down and began examining the floor; his hands searching more than his eyes for my beloved shawl.

"I can't see a thing in here!" he exclaimed after a few minutes.

I bent down to join him in his efforts but also realized how useless it was to continue searching is such a dim atmosphere.

Suddenly I felt my companion's hand grasp my arm. It was hard to distinguish Carlos' face in the darkness but I could feel the tension in his voice as he whispered, "Who's that?"

I instinctively looked straight ahead of me. The corridor was vacant except for two shadowy figures moving in from the ballroom. I could not make out their features but the one wearing a fancy pink dress seemed to be limping while being supported by the other.

The pair did not notice Carlos and me for they headed in the opposite direction; farther down the dark corridor. In the midst of their stride, the limping woman fainted and with a moan sank to the floor.

I gulped. A very strange feeling inside told me that this was more sinister than it appeared. The lady's companion bent down and gently tried to pick her up - along with the abundantly flowing dress. Finally, the person swept the lady up effortlessly and continued down the corridor.

As I watched, it seemed as if the couple was headed toward the garden entrance near the back. I was wrong. Instead, they vanished in a small door to the left.

My back was stiff and my hands had become sweaty. Only when a high pitched violin sounded from the Rose Ballroom orchestra did my mind release its heated concentration. I breathed a sigh and looked over at Carlos.

"We can look for my shawl some other time."

The boy nodded and tried to sound steady, "Yeah sure."

Carlos and I walked back to our doorway in silence. Both of us had uneasy feelings about what we had just witnessed. The hour was late and I knew I should be getting home. Carlos (the gentleman that he is) offered to escort me there. He said it was dangerous for a young girl to walk through the streets of Lyden at night. Grateful for his offer, I accepted immediately.

Just as we were heading out to go, a nervous uproar was heard in the Rose Ballroom. Carlos and I turned to see what had caused it.

My eyes roved the ballroom, looking for the source of the commotion. My gaze rested upon Queen Tabitha. The Queen's face was pale and she was in a state of confusion and anxiousness. The Ladies in Waiting were fluttering around her trying to relieve Her Majesty's agitated state.

Since the Queen was disturbed so was the King. King Gilbert was asking his wife some questions. Her answers obviously did not satisfy him but turned his pleasant expression into one of solemn gravity. The King summoned his guards and ordered that they search the castle with haste!

The guests were very much surprised at this and one man asked, "What is going on?!" the exact question that was on my mind.

King Gilbert reseated himself on his throne and said with a strong, calming voice, "You have nothing to fear dear guests. My guards are merely making a search for something very precious to me that has somehow - disappeared. Do not worry; I'm sure they'll find it before this night is over."

This explanation seemed to settle the people somewhat.

"A lot of weird things are happening tonight," Carlos remarked.

I nodded, "Yeah, very strange."

"I wonder what the King lost."

I shrugged, "Probably a ring or something, nothing worth worrying about."

"Perhaps your right. Well, let's go."

The two of us set out for my little cottage home.

The evening night was chilly as gusts of wind blew through Lyden's deserted streets. Well, not entirely deserted. There were a few people moseying about; mostly around taverns and bars. Thank heavens there are not many establishments like those in Lyden.

Still, I pulled my hooded cloak closer to me. Carlos kept a fervent watch and guided me through the darkening town. It was not long before we had reached the sloping lilac hills.

The night's peculiar events kept haunting my thoughts. Something about it was just not right! I didn't know exactly what, but a chill went down my spine every time I thought of it. I shook my head and reasoned it was just the cool night air.

The warm lights of home greeted me as I made my way up to the cottage door. I knocked good and loud and was rewarded by the wooden door instantly swinging open.

"Thank goodness you're alright!" Mother exclaimed as she hugged me. "I was wondering where you were."

"I'm sorry - time seemed to fly so fast!"

"Well you're here now and I want you in your warm bed immediately," Mother commanded in a gentle tone. "As for you young Carlos, you have my thanks."

"Thank you madam," Carlos replied. "Now if you don't mind, I'll be going home now. Goodbye Mrs. Noble, goodbye Jacqueline."

"Bye Carlos," I said with a grin before heading up the stairs.

"Adios Carlos," Mother said with a twinkle in her eye.

Ah, my bedroom! There's just something about windy nights that makes your comfy bed more inviting! I snuggled deep under the covers and with a contented sigh, closed my eyes. But sleep did not come so easily. I tossed and turned a few times before the overpowering spell of sweet sleep fell over me.

Waking up the next morning was like coming upon a new world. The dark, windy hills were now peaceful and flooded with sunshine. The whispering willow trees were at rest and there appeared not a cloud in the sky. I sat up and yawned long and hard. I stretched out my legs and arms and then sleepily wiped my eyes.

"Well, another day," I murmured.

When I got downstairs, my drowsy eyes were not unnoticed by Mother - though I tried to hide it.

"I don't want you going out late anymore. It's very unhealthy especially for a girl who must get up so terribly early for her job," Mother stated as she poured oatmeal into my bowl.

"Then why did you let me go?"

"I wanted you to enjoy yourself. You have been working very hard Jacqueline."

"I know, but it's not that bad."

Mother smiled at my positive attitude, "I'm glad you think so."

It was a sad business reporting to Phillip that I had no slice of cake to bring him. At first he went into the depths of depression - what a loss! However, when I mentioned that I would bring him something delicious from work, the little boy returned to his buoyant self!

The town's bustle was the same as the day before, but when I entered the servants' courtyard in the palace, it was as quiet as a tomb.

I could here the echo of my footsteps as I walked across the open area and up the stairs leading to the Queen's grand hall. The place looked the same and yet. . .something was different. It was the atmosphere. A dreadful heaviness seemed to linger in the air as I passed all of the east wing's rich rooms and took a peek into the center area of the palace.

"Something has happened," a voice behind me uttered.

I whirled around. It was Lin.

Chapter Seven

A Royal Crime

"What happened?" I asked.

She took my hand and led me up the white marble staircase and into the Queen's drawing room. A stylish door connected the drawing room to the Queen's bedroom, and through this door's keyhole I saw a sad sight.

Queen Tabitha was sitting on her bed, handkerchief in hand. The Ladies in Waiting were not present, but King Gilbert sat on the royal bed next to his wife. He seemed to be trying to console her.

"It is alright my dear, I will send the sum. Nothing will happen to her because she is very valuable." King Gilbert's hand clutched a letter.

"But how could this happen!" cried the Queen. "How could she have been kidnapped in front of so many people?"

"I am as bewildered as you are darling, but, it is not in our power to act now except to do what this villain has asked."

"Oh my poor, poor daughter!" sobbed Her Majesty.

The King put his arm comfortingly about his wife and after a few minutes left the room with a determined stride.

My face backed away from the keyhole and turned to Lin in amazement. "The Princess has been kidnapped?!"

Lin nodded solemnly.

"How?! When?! By whom?!" I cried in a whisper.

"No one has any answers. The King received a letter this morning saying that if he didn't give the kidnapper a certain large sum of money, Princess Vanessa would be destroyed."

"And where did you here this?" I asked with eager eyes.

"Just a few minutes ago, before you got here. I was listening in the same way you did."

"I wonder why the King isn't going public with this. I mean, shouldn't everyone be informed so they can keep a lookout for the criminal?"

Lin shrugged, "King Gilbert wants only his wife and the guards to know. Perhaps he doesn't want the people to panic - capturing a princess shouldn't have been so easy."

I nodded, "I see."

"But it is rather dreadful isn't it?" Lin said with a hint of a smile.

"You seem amused."

"Well, it isn't a shock that Princess Vanessa fell into such an unfortunate business - a temper like hers! Plenty of people want to take revenge on her. Maybe even, you."

"Don't be ridiculous," I said with a laugh, "Princess Vanessa is a pain but I would never want to kidnap her - for heaven's sake! Then she would be with me all the time!"

Lin smiled and shook her head, "Yeah well, I do feel bad for her."

"I can tell," I replied lifting an eyebrow.

Lin gave me an innocent look, "Please don't assume that I think it was right to kidnap the Princess."

"Well, whoever did do it certainly won't agree with you," I said knitting my brows together. My mind raced back, trying to think of a time I had seen Princess Vanessa during the ball. The only thing I could distinctly remember was when she had flirted with a few men from the Lydonian Marines. Surely none of them could have taken her. No, that was unlikely. Then who could it be?!

Suddenly, the creak of an opening door sounded in the drawing room.

Startled, Lin and I dove behind a sofa.

"I really need to stop eavesdropping," I murmured. From behind the couch I saw the skirt and shoes of the person who entered. Without a doubt it was Miss Hilda Primpette. I had taken a certain dislike to her lately.

The lady merely paused at the doorway and looked around the room. With a dissatisfied face she turned around and slammed the door, "Where are all the maids?! I need them to clean the Queen's bedroom!"

Lin and I looked at each other.

"If we volunteer to clean Queen Tabitha's room, perhaps we can find more information," I suggested; energized by the rush of adventure flowing through my veins.

"How will we get more information?" Lin asked.

"I don't know, but let's do it!"

We both scurried out from behind the sofa and ran after Miss Primpette.

The Head Supervisor immediately sent us up to Her Majesty's bedroom once we volunteered. "It will do you amateurs some good!" she declared.

The Queen was not occupying the bedroom when we entered it.

The bed was tussled, the curtains drawn in, and both the dresser and desk were a mess. I set about making the bed while Lin tried to organize the desk and dresser.

The fine white linen sheets seemed so soft and comfortable as I smoothed them out and tucked them in. Just as I was putting the last plush pillow in place, a piece of paper slid out.

I picked it up and unfolded the paper. It was a letter. As I read it my eyes widened. "Lin! Come look at this!"

My friend hurried over and came up beside me, "The ransom note!"

"Yes!"

"Read it!"

I cleared my throat, *"Dear King Gilbert,*

I have the great pleasure of addressing this note of ransom to you. It is concerning the return of your daughter, Princess Vanessa. In order to receive this reward you must give me something in return. I demand 2 million pounds in gold on Wednesday afternoon at precisely 1:35 p.m.. Leave the money under the shade of the large willow tree located in the Stallion's Meadow on the palace grounds. Do not have your guards accompany you or the life of the Princess will end. After you have rested the money in the assigned area leave the meadow and go back to the castle. In about ten minutes or so, your daughter will be returned. In the meantime, have a good day Sir."

"Two million pounds in gold!" Lin cried in astonishment.

"Well, it *is* the Princess."

"But come on! That's a lot of money even for a King to spend! Who could this daring villain be?"

"Probably a woman," I replied studying the letter.

"Excuse me?"

"I said a woman. Look at this letter's handwriting. It is penned by a female no doubt."

"So a woman wrote it - that doesn't help us considering that tons of women live in Lydonia."

"I don't think our criminal lives very far," I remarked with a sly grin. "It says to leave the money under a willow tree in the Stallion's Meadow which is located on the castle grounds. No one is allowed on the castle grounds except people that work here."

"So you think the person who kidnapped Princess Vanessa works *inside* the palace?! What a traitorous wretch!" Lin exclaimed; firmly placing her hands on her hips.

"I agree." My eyes once again fell on the neatly written note. It was indeed a very unfortunate affair. The poor King and Queen! Perhaps they will now realize that family stability is very essential. As for Princess Vanessa. . .well, I encouraged a faint hope that she would learn from this circumstance.

My conscience didn't allow me to keep the traitorous letter, so I placed it on the Queen's desk.

Lin and I quickly finished cleaning Her Majesty's bed-room (I felt we were getting quite good at the job) and proceeded to ask Miss Primpette for more instructions.

"You're done already?" the Head Supervisor exclaimed with a raised eyebrow.

Lin and I nodded.

Miss Primpette set her hands on her hips, "Well, I'm impressed. You two take to this job quickly."

I felt a flush of pride at these words since they came from the person who tried to punish me in front of the Queen yesterday. "Hopefully now I have a chance of keeping this job," I said to myself.

Miss Primpette assigned us our duties for the morning and then walked off with her head held high.

"You know," Lin remarked as we were mopping the glossy floor, "I wouldn't be surprised to find that Miss Primpette kidnapped the Princess."

I smiled wryly, "I wouldn't put it past her. Still, what could Miss Primpette possibly have to do with Princess Vanessa?"

"Everything!" Lin exclaimed. "I am shocked you have never considered her a possible suspect. She is suspicious, proud, sharp, and always around the royal family. Remember last night when you said Miss Primpette caught you peeking through one of the Queen's private doors. What was *she* doing there I ask you? I believe Miss High and Mighty was trying to spy on the Queen."

"Like we were doing," I remarked with a half grin.

Lin gave a little laugh, "You are right, but our intentions weren't anything but innocent curiosity."

"We shouldn't judge anyone's intentions. However, Miss Primpette is a very likely suspect."

Lin seemed satisfied that I agreed with her. We continued scrubbing for a while until I spotted Edna coming in our direction carrying a tray. By the time I had shouted, "The floor's wet Edna!" it was too late.

The elderly maid went flying! The tray and its contents whooshed up into the air!

Poor Edna, her feet catapulted her onto the floor and landed the maid firmly on her old behind.

The maid sat stunned for a while, trying to articulate in her mind what had just happened.

I quickly helped Edna to her feet while Lin went around trying to collect all the things that had spilled.

"Are you alright?" I asked.

"If you consider a sixty seven year old lady slipping and falling alright - then yes I am." Edna wrenched her arm away from my hand and straitened the mob cap on her head. "You girls could have warned me."

"I did!" I exclaimed in defense. "At any rate we're sorry we didn't warn you sooner."

Lin handed the elderly maid her tray and things.

With an indignant huff, Edna strutted out of the room.

"For some reason I don't think Edna kidnapped the Princess. She might have had a heart attack from the effort," Lin remarked.

We returned to our work and made a point of not talking about the crime - yeah right!

No matter how hard we tried to have a normal conversation, the subject just kept coming up. The presence of gloom still hung about the palace as we dusted and cleaned the lavish rooms. Our eyes were constantly watching the different women of the palace; trying to find which one had the nerve to kidnap Princess Vanessa.

But though the King and Queen may have been distressed, the rest of the workers weren't. In fact they looked almost happy that their torturer was gone! Yes, they felt badly, but it is my private opinion that they were relishing in the restful moments.

While Lin and I were shining a piano in the music room, Edna entered and informed, "Miss Primpette thinks the Queen could use some cheerful flowers. Go get them."

"It looks like it's going to rain," Lin commented looking out the window at the menacing clouds.

"Not my problem," Edna remarked with a smile.

I gave a sigh, "I'll get them."

"You don't have to Jacqueline, I'll get them."

"It's okay Lin," I replied and with a meaningful look at Edna I added, "I don't mind getting wet."

Edna gave another one of her sniffs and walked out.

I made my way to the graceful veranda and looked out upon the gardens. I breathed deeply the fresh misty air. Yes, it would definitely rain.

I hurried out to the rich green grass and flowery shrubs. The roses Mr. Fairday had picked a few days ago had to be around here somewhere.

My eyes scanned the area. Just as I spotted the lovely plants a few yards away, it began to pour.

Heavy rain droplets drenched my dress and ran down my face. It was getting hard to see now. Surely Mother wouldn't approve of me being out like this and getting soaked.

I ran up to the flowers and bent down to pick them. "Hope these make Her Majesty happy," I remarked grudgingly. I clutched the vines and gave a yank. Oh the pain!!

I instantly sprang back and cringed. I looked at my hand through the downpour. It was scarred and bloody.

"Darn thorns!" I cried.

My tears mingled with the rain as I looked helplessly around for some shelter. The gazebo in the forest came to mind, however, it would be too hard to find in the rain.

My gaze shifted to my right. Warm lights flickered in a large building. The Royal Stables! I was near it. With haste I ran to the inviting warmth.

My shoes were covered with mud as I approached the entrance to the stables. A few men were lying about in the doorway and watched me run through the rain into the dry building.

"What idiots, they don't even come out and help me," I murmured and quickened my pace until I came upon Carlos's ladder. I was not in a good mood and the stinging cuts on my hand hurt more than ever.

Here I paused for breath. My hand burned and my clothes were dripping wet. "I've been so stupid," I remarked.

"Jacqueline, is that you?" asked a warm deep voice.

I looked up the ladder and recognized the gentle face of Mr. Fairday.

I smiled with relief, "Yes, it's me. I was trying to get some roses for Queen Tabitha but it ended up raining so. . ."

"Don't say another word about it," Mr. Fairday said kindly. He helped me up the ladder and into the warm loft. Quickly the elderly gentleman took some white cloth and wrapped it around my bleeding hand. "It should be as right as rain in no time," he remarked with a merry twinkle in his eyes.

I smiled back.

A moment later Carlos came up the ladder, "So Mr. Fairday. . .Jacqueline!"

"Surprised to see me?" I said with a grin.

"Yeah! What are you doing here? Got caught in the rain?"

"No kidding," I remarked sarcastically.

"Now, now Jacqueline, take it easy," Mr. Fairday reminded with a smile.

"I don't blame her. I hate rain too," Carlos said removing his coat and shaking his glossy wet hair.

"Did you guys hear the news?" I asked sitting down on a bale of hay.

"Who hasn't," Carlos answered soberly.

Mr. Fairday nodded and looked thoughtful.

"The King wants to keep it quiet," I said.

"Good luck with that," the gardener remarked.

We all became silent as the sound of rain filled our ears.

"You know Jacqueline, I've been thinking about what we saw last night in the corridor," Carlos began.

I leaned forward eagerly, "Yeah, and?"

"Well, I don't know about you, but it struck me as very peculiar." He leaned in closer with shining eyes, "What if we were actually witnessing Princess Vanessa being kidnapped!"

I started at the notion! Why hadn't I thought of that before? It seemed probable enough.

My mind raced back, trying to remember details from that night. The flash of a sparkly pink gown blinked in my memory. The Princess had been wearing a pink gown. What if Carlos' assumption was true? I got goose-bumps just thinking about it.

"What did you two see last night?" Mr. Fairday asked with interest.

"We saw someone leading a certain lady away from the ball. It looked as if the girl was drunk or about to faint. The other person appeared to be trying to hide the girl from public attention. When the poor girl finally collapsed, her companion bent down and picked her up," Carlos explained.

"And these people didn't see you?" Mr. Fairday asked.

"It was a dark corridor and they were turned in the opposite direction. Jacqueline and I were looking for a shawl she lost."

A familiar anxiousness took hold of me again. "Oh yeah, I still have to tell Mother it's gone missing."

"Was this girl's mysterious companion a man or a woman?" Mr. Fairday pondered out loud.

Before Carlos could voice his opinion I replied, "It was a woman."

"How do you know?" the stable boy asked surprised.

"Lin and I read the ransom note this morning."

"You what!!" they both exclaimed at once.

I smiled with pleasure at having the utmost attention of my listeners, "Yes. King Gilbert left it in the Queen's bedroom. As Lin and I were cleaning the bedroom we sneaked a peek at the note. It was definitely written by a woman." I went on to explain what the ransom letter had demanded. Both my listeners sat on the edge of their seats as I told them the details.

"I don't like it," Mr. Fairday said shaking his head. "This means that someone in the castle is a traitor - a wolf in sheep's clothing."

Carlos's dark eyes sparkled with adventure, "I wish I could get my hands on him!"

"Her."

"Right, her."

"Well, I best be gettin a move on. The sun's coming out again." Mr. Fairday stood up and brushed off his trousers. "See you kids later."

"Bye Mr. Fairday."

When the gardener had gone, Carlos turned to me with eager eyes, "If the traitor is a woman, who do you think it could be?"

I shrugged, "Who knows." I stood up from the bale of hay, "I should go too."

"You have to leave now?" Carlos whined.

"I didn't know you enjoyed my company so much."

"Don't flatter yourself - I just need your help to solve the crime."

"I'm not so sure we will. I'll bet the King has put professionals on the case already."

Carlos grunted, "Professionals. What a bunch of bananas!"

I smiled and started down the ladder, "See you later amigo."

The clouds were just parting in the sky when I came to the stable's entrance.

My hand felt much better, but I dreaded the thought of cleaning the castle with it. Ouch!

I walked on through the beautiful gardens; the dewy grass brushing lightly on my legs. A few rays of sun penetrated the clouds as heavy droplets of water slid off flower petals like diamond jewels. A smile came to my face as I thought of how God created every little thing. However, my smile faded when I met Lin's tense face on the veranda.

"Thank goodness you're okay!" she said upon seeing me. "I got so worried when you didn't come back and it started to rain." She caught a glimpse of my bandaged hand. "What happened?! Are you alright?"

"I'm fine Lin, it's just a scratch." I went on to explain what had happened and about the weird incident during the ball.

"That must have been creepy, watching the crime take place and not even knowing it," Lin commented.

"Yeah. Want to check out the same corridor?"

"Jacqueline!"

"What?"

"I can't believe you want to explore that horrid scene again."

"Why not? I'm feeling a bit overly adventurous and I want to see if the kidnapper left any clues."

"Well, Miss Primpette wasn't pleased when you didn't show up with the roses for Queen Tabitha. She says you don't listen to instruction. If I were you, I'd be more careful."

My jaw tightened. What right did Miss Primpette have to judge me? It was all a mistake! I got caught in the rain! My mind raced to Phillip. How would he continue in school if I lost my job?

"God, please help me show Miss Primpette that I am responsible. Please help me keep this job," I prayed silently.

As we entered the grand hall Lin and I nearly bumped into the Ladies in Waiting.

"Watch where you're going little misses!" Charlotte snapped.

"You needn't be so prickly Charlotte, after all, Princess Vanessa isn't around to worry us," Kelsey remarked with a smirk.

I watched with disgust as they skipped away giggling.

"Such silly airheads," I said under my breath. The thought crossed my mind that one of them might have kidnapped the Princess. It wasn't a completely ridiculous notion.

"If you want to go see the corridor do it now. It's our lunch break," Lin informed.

"Are you coming with me?"

"Sure, why not."

We started down the center hall of the castle and proceeded to the Rose Ballroom.

However, before we got there, we met Mr. Jacob Monroe coming in our direction.

"Good afternoon ladies," he hailed.

We both curtseyed, "Good day to you Mr. Monroe."

"I trust the news about the poor Princess hasn't disturbed you much."

"Not very," I replied forcing a smile.

"Don't worry my dears, the King's guards will find the culprit soon enough. It shall be a glorious thing watching the villain come to justice."

Lin and I both smiled and agreed to this. My gaze then fell on a beautiful object in Mr. Monroe's pocket. It was my shawl! My eyes became big with the realization.

Feeling Mr. Monroe's eyes on me I held my countenance. But it was too late for he had discerned my sudden interest.

He reached in his pocket, "I found this in the left corridor around the Rose Ballroom last night. Does it belong to one of you?"

"Yes, as a matter of fact it belongs to me. I lost it last night." I thanked him.

"Well it is a lucky thing I picked it up," Mr. Monroe replied handing me the lovely fabric.

My hands clutched the shawl gratefully. All of a sudden, an idea struck me. How did Mr. Monroe see my shawl in the darkness of the corridor? It was rather puzzling. I wanted to ask the handsome man how he could have seen my shawl but he was off with great haste saying that he was needed elsewhere at the moment.

"Wow, if there ever was a real Prince Charming that would be him," Lin remarked with a smile as we watched the gentleman walk away.

"Please don't tell me you're held captive by his charm too," I said with a grin.

"No, not yet – but he is quite irresistible! Don't look at me that way Jacqueline Noble, I know you've thought the same thing."

"I would never!" I replied with a provoking grin.

Lin gave me a playful push. "Anyway, you should be happy. Your Mother can't punish you now that the shawl is safe."

"I still have to tell her I lost it."

"No you don't."

"Yes I do!"

"Why? It will only get you punished."

"I have to tell because it's what Jesus would do," I replied falteringly.

Lin became silent and said no more.

We both walked down the castle halls and found ourselves at the entrance to the royal kitchen. The aroma of delicious foods made our stomachs growl and led us into the kitchen in search of some snack.

Compared to the commotion before the ball, the kitchen was very mellow this afternoon. Delightful scents wafted from pots boiling on stoves and meats being spiced. Some spots on the wooden floor were cluttered with fresh vegetable peels and then swept up with a broom into the trash barrel. Lin and I walked through the maze of cooks to the macho stove where the Chef himself danced over a pot of steaming soup.

"He seems in a good mood, now that the Princess is gone," Lin remarked.

It was true. Chef Pastaloni appeared to be floating on clouds now that his nemesis had disappeared.

"It looks like he got revenge," I answered back.

"Do you think he could have kidnapped Her Majesty?" Lin asked reaching for a plum.

"I don't think so," I said slowly, "he doesn't exactly strike me as the female type."

Lin tried to contain her laughter but in vain. The Chef turned around.

"Ah! My belles! You have come to fatten your growling stomachs eh?"

Lin and I nodded with bright eyes.

"I've never heard it put that way sir but yes, we are," Lin replied.

"Good, good! Because I have a treat for you. Fresh cinnamon bread!"

"Thank you!" I said as he handed me one. He did seem awfully happy. What if he *did* commit the royal crime? My eyes watched him as he returned to work. Those big meaty hands couldn't have written in such a dainty, girly style! It couldn't be possible. . .could it?

Our lunch break was nearly over and Lin and I rushed back to work. I wasn't about to let Miss Primpette down this time.

Chapter Eight

In the Wolf's Jaws

Somehow, I finished my chores earlier than usual – a miracle! I was determined to spend this rare blessing wisely!

I did not want to leave the castle grounds just yet, so I kept my maid uniform on and went to go explore. Since the east wing was quite familiar to me, I made my way over to the west wing of the castle. It was a very long walk - who would think a building could be so large!

I came to a door gilt with gold marked West.

"I wonder whose portion of the palace this belongs to." The King owned the north wing, the Queen the east; did the Princess possess one too?

Even though my mind was made up to go in, I hesitated before opening the door. Grasping the shiny, gold handle, I shook off my growing uncertainty and swung the door wide open.

My eyes became big with pleasure as a new world of beauty opened up before me! The magnificent rooms I entered glowed with feminine splendor!

Pink sofas lounged in cream colored rooms, while sunlit breezes wafted through satin curtains and twinkling, crystal chandeliers. All things stylish and lovely could be found in the enchanting apartments I walked through! Eventually, I came to the base of a staircase decorated with peony flowers.

"This is a princess' fairyland," I murmured; for there was no doubt in my mind that this section of the palace was Princess Vanessa's quarters.

As I remembered Her Highness' unfortunate circumstance, my interest in the surrounding rooms became deeper. Thoughts of her uncommon beauty and equally hot temper filled my memories. I walked slowly through a lovely hall and into a gorgeous drawing room. A glossy wooden table stood in the center with roses and sweet pea flowers bursting forth from a glass vase. "Everything is so beautiful. How could someone live in such an atmosphere and turn out so. . ."

"Ill-tempered," a manly voice cut in.

I twirled around in utter surprise and came face to face with Jacob Monroe! I stepped back quickly.

"Mr. Monroe, you startled me," I said while maintaining a cordial curtsey.

His pleasant, handsome eyes seemed unusually icy, "Forgive me, I was just on my way out."

Perhaps it was my unprepared feelings that made me ask suddenly, "What are you doing in Princess Vanessa's private quarters?"

The man's mouth gave a slight smile, "I believe the question should be, why are *you* in Princess Vanessa's quarters? As I recall you are assigned to be the Queen's maid."

I suddenly felt embarrassed and my cheeks felt warm. "I was merely curious. You see, I am off of work now and I was just. . ."

"It is not becoming for a young lady to be in places she is not allowed," he cut in shortly.

I was stunned, ashamed, and confused, "I beg your pardon sir, but according to rules, all maids have the liberty to enter any wing of the palace. However, I am surprised you are here."

I thought I saw his color heighten. He averted his gaze with vexed disdain, "It is improper to ask the business of your superiors."

I slowly looked away in dejection.

Somewhat satisfied with my silent submission, he turned on his heel and left.

I stood there baffled, humiliated, and slightly angry. His tone, his behavior! It was so different from the dashing, gallant person the entire castle had fallen in love with!

I wondered what could have altered him. In a few seconds I heard the west doorway close.

"Why was he so irritated with me?" I pondered. At this moment, my eye caught sight of a person walking swiftly passed a nearby, open window.

I kept my gaze fixed on the spot as a soft breeze rustled the curtains. I could have sworn that the person was the man I had just talked to.

I moved closer to the window and looked out upon a vast green area where majestic horses grazed peacefully.

My attention finally centered on a person striding quickly through the calm landscape. Even from this distance, I discerned that the man was indeed Mr. Monroe.

How he had left the palace and entered the meadow so suddenly startled me; but, I suppose Mr. Monroe knew many of the palace's shortcuts that I did not.

"He's certainly going somewhere important," I remarked to myself; noting the gentleman's purposeful stride.

Suspicions began dancing in my mind as I observed his figure from the window. Even though the Princess' kidnapper was a woman, she could have had an accomplice – perhaps a very attractive, loyal, unsuspicious accomplice. . . ..named Jacob Monroe?

As I thought more about this idea, it began to appear less ridiculous and more probable. Yes! Mr. Monroe definitely could be helping the villain! After all, no one is above suspicion, right? With this juicy assumption fresh in my mind, I set off with energy through the west wing and to the meadow; intending to follow my suspect.

I hurried out of the west wing and was making my way out of the castle when Lin suddenly appeared and grabbed my arm.

"What are you doing and where are you going?" she asked with surprise.

I was in a rush! He could have disappeared by now! "If you must know, I am on the trail of a possible accomplice to Princess Vanessa's kidnapper. I have to go now or I'll lose sight of him."

"Him?!" Lin exclaimed.

"Yes, Mr. Monroe."

"Oh Jacqueline, your insane!" Lin scolded. "Of all the people you would pick to be a villain! Mr. Jacob Monroe is the handsomest, kindest gentleman I've ever met - he wouldn't hurt a fly! What evidence do you have?"

I smiled slyly, "Just hunch, a pretty big one that grows the more I think about it."

Lin stood with her hands on her hips and gave me a daunting look, "Are you really going after him?"

"Yes, with or without you!" I declared and rushed out the door.

"Fine! Then I'm coming with you!" Lin groaned with exasperation.

Both of us ran through the evening dusk to the lush, grassy meadow. We didn't want Mr. Monroe to see us, so we stayed a good pace behind him; hiding behind bushes and trees every once in a while.

As we spied on the debonair gentleman, a certain rush of excitement took over me as I realized that this was an adventure - a real, true adventure! I had read about this kind of stuff in books, but never really believed it could actually happen to me!

It was obvious that Lin was catching the feeling too for she moved with a stealthy step and attentive eyes.

After a while, we realized that Mr. Monroe was not in the Stallion's Meadow but was in fact heading toward the entrance of the palace.

"What on earth is he doing? Are we going to follow him out of the castle?" Lin asked.

I nodded, "Oh yeah."

Since it was time for the maids to leave anyway, Lin and I returned our uniforms, ran out of the servant's courtyard and onto the road to the town.

Everybody was returning from their day's work so the streets were crowded and it was extremely difficult keeping Mr. Monroe in sight.

"He could just be heading home - which is what *we* should be doing!" Lin commented as the crowd thickened.

Perhaps Lin was right. We should go home. I paused in the street and waited for her to catch up. But what was that?! In a flash, I had caught a glimpse of a man who looked like Mr. Monroe; and he was heading straight down a dark alley.

"Come on Lin! Just one more look and we'll be done sleuthing for today." I pointed at the alley.

Lin sighed, "Alright."

We pushed our way through the throng of people to the alley's entrance. It was a dark, grimy sort of place that was narrowed by two large, looming buildings on both sides. These two structures had entrances into this alley that were covered by rugged, worn doors. The manly figure of Mr.

Monroe walked a few paces down and then disappeared into a black painted door.

"Alright, you said one peek, now let's go," Lin whispered; a vague tone of anxiety in her voice.

"We're not done with our look yet. Come on," I urged.

With a determined gulp, Lin followed me into the mysterious unknown.

A few dusty, dirty windows looked into the alley from the two gloomy buildings. Lin and I watched our steps carefully; avoiding trash. The twilight sky was darkening by the minute.

I stared at the black painted door. Should I go inside? I wanted to ask Lin but I knew all she would give me was an anxious 'no' so I restrained myself.

Despite my efforts for courage, my hand started shaking the instant it took hold of the knob. "No, don't do it! You have no idea what's behind there!" a voice inside me warned.

I heard Lin's faint moan of fear behind me.

I tightened my jaw and turned the knob. "We'll just see if it opens," I told her.

Unfortunately, it opened a little too well. With my slight effort, and a gust of wind blowing through the alley, the black door opened wide.

Lin and I found ourselves staring into a small, old foyer that led into a side room, a narrow hall, and a down a flight of stairs.

"It would be a shame to come this far and not go in, right?" I exclaimed to Lin; trying to mask my nervousness.

"I see no shame in turning back!" Lin replied in a harsh whisper.

"Lin, we could be on the verge of saving the Princess of our country!"

"I'm sorry, but the opportunity to save a brat doesn't inspire me," Lin answered dryly.

I took Lin's hand and gave her a look of encouragement. Turning to the open door, I stepped inside.

Our shoes were muffled slightly by the worn carpet. I looked around at the dreary, bare walls and the empty room that led off from the foyer. Down the hall, I distinguished the flickering light of a candle.

"I don't think he lives here," I whispered to Lin.

She agreed silently.

Just then, faintly, I heard voices coming from down the hall where the light was.

A gruff man exclaimed, "Is this your way of paying me back? You idiot! You'll be shot dead or arrested before you have my money!"

"Relax Martin. If you can settle down and at least *act* smart for once, you'll get more than your share."

"Don't test me Monroe! I have the nerve to either butcher you or betray your wild scheme!"

"No, you don't," I heard Mr. Monroe reply coldly.

Before I could catch any more of their talk, Lin nudged my arm and motioned to the basement stairs.

"I think someone's down there and they're hurt," Lin whispered.

Moving closer to the stairway, moans of irritation and pain reached my ears. Without asking Lin's consent, I immediately started down the stone steps. I heard her following close behind.

The smell of a musty, dank cellar filled my senses and I saw Lin's face grimace with disgust. I too, was thinking of heading back upstairs and out of this dangerous situation.

But then, I saw something that made me freeze in my tracks.

In the far left corner of the room, a huddled figure was illuminated by the ghostly light of a single, half melted candle. Wrapped in a beautiful pink gown, with harsh ropes tied around her wrists, legs, and ankles, sat the Princess herself.

I started back aghast and Lin let out a little scream!

It all rushed on me in an instant – Jacob Monroe wasn't an accomplice. . . .he was the kidnapper!!

At that moment we heard footsteps and an exclamation from above.

I turned to Lin but she was already halfway up the stairs.

In a panic I had never experienced before, I hastened up the cellar stairs and into the dingy foyer. Throwing the door open I jumped outside to see Lin skid to a stop and beckon insistently, "C'mon! Quickly!"

The next thing I felt was a hand yank my collar so tightly I nearly choked. The person started to go for Lin but she sped away and ran down the alley faster than a comet!

I turned around to see the frightening face of Mr. Monroe.

"Let me go!" I attempted to scream but his hand clutched my jaw and tightened its grip. I winced as the pain shot through my head like a lightning bolt.

His steely eyes glared at me. I met his gaze with a defiant stare.

That was a bad choice.

He took hold of my neck and thrust me to the wall. I gasped for breath as his fingers dug into my skin.

"I knew there was something wrong with you the first time I met you," he breathed. "You incompetent, nosy little snip!"

Tears escaped my eyes as I strained to get out the words, "Please, please don't kill me!" Sweat beads came down my forehead.

He seemed to consider a moment. His wicked eyes became a little calmer as he put his face directly into mine, "If you even begin to breathe a word of what you've seen tonight I will kill you – and your family."

My heart nearly stopped at the words and for a second, I thought I would surely die. My lips quivered and I could feel myself becoming lightheaded. I needed oxygen!

"Got it?!" he threatened.

My eyes filled with tears as I feebly nodded my head.

He finally released his grip and I sank to the floor coughing and gasping for fresh air!

My whole body was shivering and my hands grasped for something to hold onto. My throat hurt terribly so I didn't dare attempt to speak.

My eyes fluttered open and I looked up into the face of Mr. Monroe. For the first time, I noticed he looked uncomfortable and uncertain while gazing down at me. Apparently, he was waiting for me to stand up.

I made an attempt to sit up and succeeded.

Mr. Monroe extended his hand to help me up but I avoided it with wary eyes. I stood up and kept my frightened gaze on him. Taking a chance I bolted from the alley and ran. . .ran. . .ran!

I can scarcely remember a more horrid, wild eyed night than that one!

While I ran, every now and then I would glance behind to see if the villain was following me through the night.

Thank God he didn't.

I did not stop for breath until I was at the front of my cottage home. I sat down on the soft grass and made an attempt to calm myself. My throat didn't hurt that much anymore, so I massaged it with my fingers while making an effort to speak. Thankfully, I could still talk.

I did not want Mother seeing me in such a state of distress so I smoothed out my hair and took in deep breaths. My weary eyes gazed up at the night sky filled with sparkling stars. Peace. I inhaled and exhaled the refreshing night air.

Even though I wished to avoid it, a flood of thoughts and questions filled my mind.

Should I tell Mother what I had just been through? Would it put her in greater danger? Probably not, though I hated the idea that it might. It wasn't even possible to tell anyone else; 'Prince Charming' would certainly be on my tail if I did.

What about Lin? I would have to explain to her at least, because she was there. I covered my head with my hands; an enormous pressure weighed on my soul that I had never felt before. It was terrible - aggravating even! My head was in a whirl! What should I do?!

Ah! Nothing is more tortuous than the stress of indecision.

I finally decided to do the right thing and tell Mother. I took comfort in hoping that I wouldn't be facing this catastrophe alone.

I yawned long and hard and finally realized how exhausted I was.

I knocked weakly on the wooden cottage door and it was opened warmly by Mother.

"Jacqueline, are you alright?" was the first thing that came out of her mouth. You can never fool her.

I was about to blurt it all out when Phillip came around, his bright face smiling up at me.

"I'm. . .okay," I replied.

"Did you bring me something good to eat?!" my little brother asked hopefully.

I touched my brown bag and found that it was still slung over my shoulder. My face broke out into a grin, "Yes I did." And with that, I pulled out some gingerbread cake from the royal kitchen.

Brimming with boundless joy, Phillip grabbed it and ran to the kitchen table to devour the sugar filled treat. "Thanks Jackie!!"

"Come, sit down with me darling," Mother said ushering me inside the cozy cottage. "You look exhausted."

"I feel exhausted," I replied slumping down into a chair near the living room fireplace.

Mother pulled up the rocking chair and began knitting beside me. Phillip didn't pay any attention to either of us.

With a brief glance at Phillip, Mother finally asked, "So, what is troubling you?"

I took a deep sigh and then spilled out the entire story. I explained everything from the moment Mr. Monroe and I met in the West Wing to the finale in the alley.

Mother just stared at me; shock and worry written all over her face.

I couldn't bear to see her face in such a state so I made myself busy twirling a piece of loose yarn from the blanket covering the couch. After a few minutes I felt Mother's loving arms wrap around me tightly and tears fall from her face.

Her voice was choked with emotion as she exclaimed, "I'm so glad you're safe! Oh praise God!" she cried softly.

A release came over me as I rested in her arms. For a few sweet moments, my fear and anxiety melted away. Unfortunately, the moments were *few*.

Soon, Mother began pacing the room and thinking aloud of what to do next.

"What to do!" I nearly cried. "Isn't it obvious? We can't tell anyone or we'll die!"

"Even though that's true, we must find a way to tell the King and Queen. It's the right thing to do," Mother declared with hesitant firmness. "Besides, Mr. Monroe may have only been trying to intimidate you. If he's desperate for money, than he probably doesn't have the resources to follow through with his threats."

"Or, he's an accomplished criminal who can do what he boasts," I retorted.

"That is also possible," Mother stated bitterly.

"How can you even think of reporting Mr. Monroe to the King?!" I exclaimed hotly. "The risk. . ."

"Jacqueline! Please, you're not making this any better!" Mother cried. "We *must* tell the authorities! It is our duty as citizens of Lydonia and followers of Christ."

I sat back down in my seat and the room lapsed into an unsettled silence.

"Couldn't we just wait until King Gilbert has given Mr. Monroe the money and Princess Vanessa is safe?" I said faintly.

Mother sat down next to me with a sigh and covered her face with her hand. Lifting her head she turned to me and kissed my forehead.

"I'm scared Mother," I whispered as I leaned on her shoulder.

"I know darling. . .I know."

"What's going on?" Phillip finally asked from the kitchen.

"Nothing dear. Why don't you go upstairs and get ready for bed. I'll be up to kiss you goodnight," Mother said with a wan smile.

"Okay," he said and gave each of us a smooch on the cheek.

When little Phillip was upstairs, Mother said quietly, "I will go and report Mr. Monroe to the King and Queen tomorrow."

"What! No! You can't!" I cried standing up.

"Settle down darling."

"If you go to the castle, Mr. Monroe will get suspicious and either harm you or flee the country with the Princess! Then how will the authorities find him?"

Mother took my hand, "What other choice is there? I'm certainly not going to put *you* in danger and ask *you* to tell the Queen! The best way for us to do this is if I tell the Queen without alerting Mr. Monroe."

I shook my head, "Mr. Monroe might not be surprised to see me working there, but he certainly won't be happy if he sees you."

"Then I will have to pray that God closes his eyes to my entrance," Mother stated as she stood up and walked over to the kitchen. I watched her put meat and vegetables on my plate and then motion me over. "Eat, you must be hungry."

I was in a state of anxious distress and could hardly swallow a thing. Mother sat opposite of me in quiet contemplation.

After a time, I felt her eyes on me and I looked up to meet her gaze.

"Jacqueline, there might be another solution."

I sat up attentively.

"You mentioned that Mr. Monroe would not be surprised if you went to the palace for work. Well, what if you did your duties as a maid, and at some time, went and told the Queen about what happened. It would be less dangerous if you told Her Majesty than me, because Mr. Monroe wouldn't expect you to do such a thing after his terrible threats."

Well, I did not like this idea at all. Me? Tell the Queen? No way!

I shook my head nervously, "That won't work either. I'd still be in danger – he can keep his eye on me at the palace."

"But it *is* safer and I believe that you can do it! God will be with you," Mother encouraged.

I firmly refused and in a fumbling voice tried to explain that the Queen might not even believe me and that Mr. Monroe would rip me to pieces if he suspected any foul play.

Mother was silent.

Scared and frustrated, I turned on my heel and quickly took refuge upstairs in my room.

Never did I feel so awful in my entire life! I pulled off my day clothes with force and shoved on my night gown;

flopped in bed, and jerked the covers over me. My confusion and fear had given over to a steam of vengeful anger.

Why couldn't I have just listened to Lin and not gone down that stupid alley! Why did I let my curiosity get the better of me, then I wouldn't be in this mess! And that traitorous rat! How dare he do such things!

My heart and mind were so full of these emotions that I didn't focus enough to pray.

After several minutes of lying in a torturous state of mind, Mother gently opened the door and whispered, "Jacqueline, are you awake?"

I didn't answer.

Slowly, Mother came over and bent her head to kiss my cheek with soft tenderness. "I love you."

I bit my lip hard trying to prevent the hot tears from falling down my face, but it was no use.

Mother left the room just as quietly as she came and closed the door.

I was left alone in the dark. There was no way I was sleeping that night. My conscience wouldn't allow it.

"Oh God!" I cried softly, "help me!"

Chapter Nine

The Weight of Decision

*I*t was amazing that I got a wink of sleep that night. How do I know I slept? Well, I woke up. The fatigue from last night must have done its work.

I sat up and stretched long and hard. I rubbed my eyes and groggily moved myself out of bed.

I flung open my closet door and slipped off my night-gown. I had thrown my clothes off quite recklessly last night and now it was a pain trying to find them. After a little rummaging, I came upon the dress I wanted.

A gentle knock was heard at my door.

"Come in," I invited.

Mother opened it.

"Good morning darling. Did you sleep well?"

I nodded, "As well as a girl can under such circumstances."

"Are you feeling alright? Perhaps you shouldn't go to work today." Her voice was warm and kind.

Guilt ebbed at my conscience. "I'll be okay."

"I don't want you walking through Lyden alone so I have asked Mr. Fairday to accompany you. He will meet you at the main road," Mother informed me.

I was surprised and thankful that she had gotten up that early to do that for me. I turned grateful eyes towards her, "Thanks Mom."

She smiled back.

Before she closed the door I said, "Mom, I'm sorry for the way I acted last night. I shouldn't have gone into the alley in the first place. Please forgive me." Tears threatened to spill out on my cheeks but I restrained them.

Mother seemed to have noticed my inward suffering. She came and put her arms around me in a tight hug, "I forgive you. I love you Jacqueline. I want you to know that you don't have to go and tell the Queen – I will do it."

Tears escaped my eyes, "Can you wait until I decide?"

"That all depends. When will you decide?" she asked.

"I'll have an answer by the end of the day."

Mother considered, "Alright, but no later than that. The ransom is tomorrow isn't it?"

I nodded.

"Now," Mother began when we finally parted, "I want you to seek God and ask Him what you should do."

"Can't you just tell me?" I replied.

She smiled, "No dear."

"How do I seek God?"

"Well, reading His Word certainly helps. I think it's time you grew your own, personal devotion time. Every morning, make it a goal to read at least a chapter of the scriptures. It holds all the answers to life's problems – big and small. It will strengthen your relationship with Jesus."

Even though this was new, I was determined to do what she had told me.

"Where do I start?" I asked her.

Mother thought for a moment, "Well, we have been reading the book of Esther lately. Why don't you start where we left off?"

I nodded and turned to Esther chapter four starting with verse fourteen. Mordecai sent this urgent message to Queen Esther, "For if thou altogether holdest thy peace at this time, then shall there enlargement and deliverance arise to the Jews from another place; but thou and thy father's house shall be destroyed: and who knoweth whether thou art come to the kingdom for such a time as this?

"Then Esther bade them return Mordecai this answer, 'Go, gather together all the Jews that are present in Shushan, and fast ye for me, and neither eat or drink three days, night or day: I also and my maidens will fast likewise; and so will I go in unto the king, which is not according to the law: and if I perish, I perish.'"

I bit my lip at the last words. Esther had so much courage and grace that I envied her. Was God telling me to go and share the truth with King Gilbert? My spirit felt convicted and I slowly shut the Bible. What was I to do? How was I to respond? I certainly didn't want to do this, but now I knew that I probably should do it!

I placed the Bible on the table near the rocking chair and headed for the door. I slung my brown bag over my shoulder and set out in the early morning light.

"Did the Lord speak to you?" Mother asked before I left.

I nodded and forced a smile, "Yep."

The twittering of birds sounded sweetly in the crisp morning air. My feet ran through the dewy, sloping hills to the main road leading to town. How I loved the morning! It held a certain charm that the rest of the day didn't. It gave off a bright hope of a fresh new start!

As I neared the red dirt road I saw Mr. Fairday waiting for me.

"Good morning Mr. Fairday!" I greeted with a smile.

"Good morning Miss Noble!" he saluted back with the usual merry twinkle in his eye.

Our conversation on the way to Lyden was pleasant and I was relieved that Mr. Fairday did not ask me the reason why Mother had insisted he accompany me.

As we neared the servant's courtyard, Mr. Fairday slightly bowed and replied, "It has been a great pleasure young lady, but I am afraid now we must depart."

"Thank you for your gallantry Mr. Fairday," I answered with a curtsey.

The elderly gentleman went on his way to the gardens and I made my way to the maid's entrance that led to the east wing.

In the doorway I met a panic stricken Lin.

"Jacqueline!" she exclaimed upon seeing me, "I'm so glad you're alive!"

She grasped me in a firm hug.

"It's alright Lin, I'm fine."

"Fine. . .fine! How could you say that. . ."

I motioned for her to keep her voice down, "I will tell you everything later. But, you must promise not to tell anyone."

"I promise! But you can't leave me hanging in suspense all day! Come, you must tell me now."

"Not now!"

"But. . ."

"Not now."

Lin sighed, "You're aggravating."

"Yes I am, but, you're just going to have to bear with me."

We climbed up the stairs leading to the grand hall. Following our regular routine, we dawned on our maid uniforms and set about to work.

Miss Primpette came around once in a while to check on us and see how we were doing. Sometimes she was pleased other times, she was not pleased at all. She would particularly note *my* mistakes.

Miss Primpette had a growing dislike for me that was based on misinterpreted incidents. The Princess called me the Jack Maid and I was fearful that Miss Primpette would adopt the nickname. So far she hadn't, but I was still in a state of uncertainty as to whether I would keep my job at the end of the week.

Lin was confident that she had won the lady's good opinion and would end up keeping her job. But my friend did feel sorry for me, for she couldn't give the same hopes for my situation.

I saw very little of Queen Tabitha that day. It was rumored that she had intended to stay with the King in his royal chambers which was located in the north wing. However, the Queen's absence could not hide her anxiety. I found traces of it all around her rooms. Her bed was tussled, the desk was in a mess, the pillows on couches were thrown everywhere, and the happy flowers in the glass vase had been thrown out.

"Looks like she's trying to be miserable," Lin said while staring at the empty vase.

"I don't think she feels like being cheerful," I replied picking up a crumpled nightgown from the floor.

"Still, it doesn't mean she has to mope around," Lin said.

"There's nothing else she can do," I answered.

Lin seemed surprised at my response, "Are you defending the Queen? I thought you didn't approve of her."

I shrugged, "I suppose it's harder than we think to be in such a high position of authority and responsibility." I sighed, "When you're in certain situations things can pressure you to act in a way you wouldn't have before."

Lin was looking at me intently. "Perhaps you're right. Then again, I would pronounce a person who bends with the situation to be a weakling. Only strong people stand firmly in hard circumstances."

I didn't reply. Something in Lin's words pulled the very same cord in my heart that God did when I read His word. The fact that Lin repeated the same message to me without knowing it produced a new splash of shame on my conscience.

"When are you going to tell me what happened last night?" Lin said lowering her voice so the other maids couldn't hear.

"At lunch break," I whispered back.

After a while of silence Lin exclaimed in a hushed tone, "I can't believe *he* did it."

"Who?"

"Mr. Monroe! Who else?" Lin replied.

I clenched my jaw at the name. "I don't ever want to hear the traitor's name again!"

Lin quickly became quiet and neither of us mentioned anything about 'the man' for the rest of the morning.

Lunch break came and after Lin and I grabbed some apples from Mr. Pasta's kitchen, we headed for the palace gardens. The day was bright and cheerful without a cloud in the sky. Busy bees hummed while flying from flower to flower gathering nectar; lazy butterflies rested on soft petals and then fluttered away in indignation if disturbed. Wind rustled through the green grass and blossoming trees. It was like a piece of heaven on earth. I picked some lilacs and twirled them with my fingers as thoughts went through my mind.

"So," Lin began after some moments of calm silence, "tell me everything."

I breathed a deep sigh and nodded my head, "Well, I. . ."

"Hey! Wait up!"

We turned around to see Carlos running up to us through the colorful beds of flowers.

"I saw you come out of Mr. Pastaloni's kitchen, so I came after you. What are you up to?" he asked coming into step with us.

"Nothing," Lin retorted shortly, taking a bite out of her apple.

Carlos eyed her with sharp suspicion.

Lin calmly avoided his gaze and pretended to be busy looking at the scenery.

"You're hiding something and I know it!" he exclaimed at once. He ran in front of us and threateningly remarked, "I'm not letting you go unless you tell me your secret."

"Really! You are absolutely. . ." Lin began with a lunge towards him. . .

"It's alright!" I interjected. "Carlos is our friend and we need to stick together, right?"

"That's right!" Carlos stated.

Lin looked at Carlos's vibrance with annoyance. Whispering in my ear she said, "You don't have to tell him! This information is too important!"

"You do realize I can hear you," Carlos said leaning in.

"Oh! You're impossible!" Lin replied quickly.

I rolled my eyes. Now I would *have* to tell Carlos too. I knew he wouldn't rest until he found out the truth. "I will tell both of you since you are my friends. But again, you must promise to keep silent about it. Your life could depend on it."

"You have my solemn word," Carlos replied holding up his hand.

I nodded with a smile, "Good, let's go somewhere no one will overhear us."

"Where?"

I thought a moment. "I know! The gazebo!"

So, the three of us ran through the fairytale gardens to the willow forest and eventually, entered the gazebo covered with rose vines.The lovely place was surrounded by beautiful trees and twittering birds. A thin dirt path was the only way leading to this secluded spot.

"This is quite nice!" Lin exclaimed sitting down on the ring of cushions that lined the gazebo.

"Yeah, real pretty," Carlos remarked carelessly.

I was proud of this special place. I smiled at my friends; and then, for a few peaceful moments of still quiet, breathed in the rose scented air.

"Alright! Enough pleasantries! Let's get down to business. Jacqueline, tell us what happened," Carlos urged.

I laughed, "Okay!"

And so, I went on to explain for the second time, what had happened that dreadful night.

Carlos and Lin listened to me with undivided attention until I had finished the fearsome tale.

When I ended, I looked up to see what their initial response would be.

Lin didn't say a word but worry and concern streaked her face.

Carlos's eyes were as bright as fire and his brows were knit in concentration; his jaw was set in vengeful indignation.

A few minutes of very intense silence slipped by as my two friends let the information sink in.

"The traitor!!" Carlos cried in a burst of infuriated emotion.

Lin and I both jumped in our seats at the sudden exclamation.

"So, now I find myself in a difficult situation," I said.

"Oh Jacqueline! Why did this have to happen to you, of all people? It's a miracle you weren't killed," Lin exclaimed with a slight quiver. "I wish I could have helped you somehow."

"I would've punched the villain's head off!" Carlos replied walking about the gazebo in a state of frustration.

"Well, what should I do now?" I asked.

"Is there any question?!" both of them answered at once.

"You shouldn't tell! You'll be killed!" Lin stated.

"No! She should tell!" Carlos replied turning sharply to Lin.

"Why would she do that?!" Lin asked with surprise and anger.

"Because it's the right thing to do!" Carlos answered with a heated temper.

"To do that would be suicide! For some reason, I don't see that as the *right* thing to do! In fact, it sounds rather foolish!"

"You wouldn't understand!" Carlos shot back. "God would want Jacqueline to never back out from something like this. He did the right thing even when it cost him his life! Isn't that right Jacqueline?"

He looked to me for support. I just sat there, not knowing what to say. After a few minutes I said, "Please! Just settle down! Getting all hyped up isn't helping me! You don't know how hard this is."

They each exchanged glances and meekly sat down.

"Sorry I got hyped up Jacqueline. I was just a little. . .um. . .well sorry," Carlos stated uncomfortably.

"It's okay," I murmured.

"I'm sorry too. But Jacqueline, please don't tell anyone. Just wait until it's all over. I don't want you to get hurt," Lin said squeezing my hand.

"Don't think for a minute I want you to get hurt - but justice must be done, whatever the cost. If you let this one slip by, who's to say Mr. Monroe won't try this tactic again?" Carlos pressed with earnest eyes.

I looked from one to the other. Lin's advice sounded nice, while Carlos's irritated me. Yet I felt somewhat guilty accepting Lin's advice; and though I knew Carlos's was hard,

I felt that if I didn't do it, something inside me would be messed up.

I simply sighed and my head sank into my hands in confusion.

Silence enveloped the atmosphere until all you could hear was the gentle breeze swaying through the trees and the light, musical twitter of birds.

"Well," Carlos began after a while, "I have to get back to work. Thank you for trusting me with this secret Jacqueline. I won't tell a soul."

I smiled, "You're welcome."

And with that, the stable boy strutted out of the gazebo and disappeared around the little dirt path.

I looked over at Lin. "You don't hate Carlos, do you?"

"No, I couldn't. It's impossible to hate him. But I will say that I do not agree with his passionate opinions."

I gave a little laugh.

Lin and I walked back to the castle to resume our maid duties.

The day was long and hard. I think the extra amount of pressure weighing on my mind added to the stress of labor. I felt like running away and hiding, but to expose the kidnapper and sacrifice safety sounded more heroic. "I don't want to be a hero!" I cried within myself. "I just want to survive!"

Lin and I were sweeping the dining area when she said, "You know, I think it's best if you follow your natural inclination and protect yourself and your family. It's only right that you do."

I said nothing for a while. Finally I uttered this question, "What would you say if I did reveal the truth?"

Lin continued to sweep, "I'd say you were acting foolishly and out of a human's common sense. No one in their right mind would do such a dangerous thing - even though Carlos considers it heroic."

I didn't reply. My heart knew what the right thing to do was - but the cost? It was too much.

The day ended with the sun setting beautiful colors across the vast skies. I walked across the palace to the place where I would leave my maid's outfit for tomorrow. The grand halls were nearly deserted except for an occasional maid or butler passing by.

My footsteps echoed in the magnificent hallways. The soft rays of the sunset illuminated the rooms with a gentle elegance. Everything was beautiful.

As I opened the door leading to the east wing, I came face to face with Mr. Jacob Monroe.

I gave a start and then froze, chills running through my body. My eyes stared rigidly into his face.

It was obvious he anticipated my agitation. After a few minutes of dead silence, he gave me a warm smile and tried to make me less uncomfortable (as if that was possible). With a short bow he said quietly, "Good day to you, Miss Noble."

I was too stiff that my knees couldn't bend in a curtsey - and even if I could, I wouldn't show this man such politeness! As I stared into his handsome, beguiling face, it made me wonder how such a man could be so cruel.

Responding to my mute answer with indifference, he moved past me and continued on his way.

My heart skipped a beat and my blood had run cold when he had brushed past me. I didn't dare take another look behind me. When I heard his footsteps become less and less audible, my heart rate began to slow down. I closed my eyes and breathed in to quiet myself. Oh! how I wanted to give that man a good punch! With forced composure, I continued on my way to the maids' dressing room.

When I walked out of the dressing room, I slung my bag over my shoulder and headed for the servants' courtyard.

There, I would meet Mr. Fairday and he would walk me home.

A light breeze blew the hair off my neck and swished my skirt so it moved like the waves of the sea. The sun's last warm rays shone on my face - it felt so good!

Mr. Fairday was waiting at the servant's entrance for me. The elderly man smiled when he caught sight of me.

"Hello there Jacqueline! Did you have a good day?" he asked.

"As good as it could have gone sir, thank you," I replied.

"In other words it did not go well," he stated as we started down the road.

I just shrugged. I was grateful Mr. Fairday didn't seem to need an answer.

We continued walking through the town and finally the lovely lilac hills in sweet, peaceful silence. I felt secure and happy in Mr. Fairday's presence. His quietness comforted me.

"Mr. Fairday," I spoke suddenly.

"Yes?"

"What would you do if you knew some vital evidence that need to be reported, but was too scared to do so because your life might be in danger? Is it better to keep silent and wait it out, or be stupidly courageous and just do it?"

"That's a tough one," Mr. Fairday admitted. "Well, what does the Bible say?"

"Today, I read that Esther was willing to sacrifice her life in order to relieve the Jews of their suffering. She said, 'If I perish, I perish'. But I'm not like her! I'm no beautiful, noble queen!"

"No, you don't need to be. God made you. . .you. Don't you think that the Lord purposefully had you read that passage today?" Mr. Fairday prodded.

"I tried to think that He didn't," I replied slowly.

"Well, if that's what God's word spoke to you today, then, if I were you, I would listen. The outcome of listening to the Bible is a lot better than not taking heed. I believe God had your answer all along."

I bit my lip. Was it true? Jesus had presented to me the answer from the beginning. I had thought so, but I didn't want to believe it.

With a trembling voice I replied, "You're right, sir. I guess I do know what I need to do."

A faint smile came across the elderly man's face.

We had come up to my cottage by now and just before I opened the door I looked back and said, "Thank you Mr. Fairday."

"Anytime," he replied.

I entered the cottage and was greeted warmly by my family.

After supper, I pulled Mother aside and told her of my decision.

She was quite surprised, and understood completely.

As I lay on my pillow that night, my stomach was still in knots. Tomorrow, the King would give the money to Mr. Monroe in exchange for his daughter. At least the stress of indecision was gone. Sticking to the decision was what made my stomach fluttery. But the fact that I had made the right choice gave my mind and heart at peace.

"Thank you Lord, for directing my paths. Now, please give me the strength to follow through!"

Chapter Ten

Jacqueline's Scheme

The next morning was Wednesday, May 27, 1779. I delayed getting out of bed; wishing, pretending that there was no danger ahead of me.

At precisely 1: 00 p.m. King Gilbert would make his way to the Horses Meadow and under some shady tree place a heavy bag of money then return to the castle. At this moment Mr. Monroe would release Princess Vanessa (hopefully) and take the bag of cash. It was a clear cut plan. What was I to do? Well, I have to stop the King before he enters the Stallion's Meadow and explain to him who the villain is, and where to find his hiding place. Of course, that's the plan if Mr. Monroe doesn't discover my intentions and kills me.

I didn't jump excitedly out of bed that morning. It's understandable, isn't it reader.

It didn't help things when Phillip came bursting into my room declaring that I was going to be late for work.

"Come on Jackie! Mommy has already made breakfast!" he squealed pulling the sheets off of my head.

I slowly opened my eyes and stared into his vibrant face and clear blue eyes. Why is it that every time I see his face I lose the urge to scold him? I was pretty mad at myself for it. So, without an answer, I sat up stiffly and yawned.

Phillip laughed out loud at my yawning expression. "You look so ridiculous!"

"Perhaps it's because I've been awakened from a good nights sleep by a rooster!" I remarked angrily.

Phillip shrugged and then with a cautious tone replied, "Sorry. You're not upset with me, are you?"

Again! Those pleading blue eyes!

"No," I answered, "I'm not upset, just. . .grumpy."

My little brother's face broke out into a smile, "Okay! See you downstairs!" And with that he ran out of my room, his tiny feet pattering on the floor, and down the stairs.

I stood up and stretched. "Well, might as well get this day over with."

I tried to assume a cool demeanor that would mask my fear. My hands were sweaty and wobbly as I put on my clothes. Yes, I was doing the right thing and I knew that if I died I would go to heaven but still. . . . . .I didn't want to die, not today!

I kept praying silently through my whole morning routine and came down to breakfast a nervous wreck.

There was no use even trying to hide my agitation from mother. She knew everything. But, because Phillip was present, she didn't say much about it.

I barely finished my oatmeal and trudged over to the rocking chair for my daily Bible reading in discomfort. I opened to where I had left off, Esther chapter five. I started with verse one and then read on until the last verse, "Then said Zeresh his wife and all his friends unto him, 'Let a gallows be made of fifty cubits high, and tomorrow speak thou unto the king that Mordecai may be hanged thereon: then go thou in merrily with the king unto the banquet.' And the thing pleased Haman; and he caused the gallows to be made." I gulped after reading this verse. Did Mr. Monroe signify Haman and I was Mordecai who was bound to be hanged? I shuddered.

I flipped the page to read the sixth chapter. I read of how Haman deceived and tricked the king into making a stupid law that would eliminate all the Jews. It reminded me exactly of Mr. Monroe and poor King Gilbert. Haman and Jacob Monroe are both heartless traitors. King Ahasurerus never suspected Haman of planning such a horrible scheme and I'll bet King Gilbert doesn't suspect Mr. Monroe of such a crime either.

Chapter seven spoke of the final banquet night, where Queen Esther was going to reveal the truth about Haman to the king.

Verse five says, "Then the king Ahasurerus answered and said unto Esther the queen, 'Who is he, and where is he, that durst presume in his heart to do so?' And Esther said, 'The adversary and enemy is this wicked Haman.' Then Haman was afraid before the king and the queen."

I kept reading with earnest eyes until the final verse, "So they hanged Haman on the gallows that he had prepared for Mordecai. Then was the king's wrath pacified."

I breathed in a deep sigh. What was God trying to teach me through this? I laid the Bible aside; closed my eyes and folded my hands.

"Lord Jesus," I prayed silently, "please tell me how this passage relates to me?"

My mind went over what I had just read. God was with Esther and Mordecai all along. They trusted him with everything! Then a thought flashed in my mind. What if they hadn't done the right thing and trusted God but panicked! The entire race of the Jews might not have survived! Whoa.

Then this still small voice whispered, "Trust me. Just as I was there for Esther, I will be there for you. Remember, I bless those who obey my word." I bowed my head, "Yes Lord."

I asked Jesus for the strength and grace to do the right thing completely. I got up from my knees refreshed and determined.

As I swung my brown bag over my shoulder Mother came over and kissed me goodbye.

"Are you sure you don't want me to come with you?" she asked with concern.

I shook my head, "No, if you come Mr. Monroe will get suspicious and kill me for sure. God will help me get through it."

"Very well then," Mother replied with a proud gleam in her eye, "goodbye my darling." And with another kiss and hug, I was off!

My mind was too distracted and full to heed the beautiful lilac hills or the fresh morning sky. Normally I would have smiled at the butterfly passing by, but this time, I continued on my way in sober reflection.

I went over the details of the crime in my mind. If Jacob Monroe committed the kidnap, then who had written that lovely, womanly, ransom note to the King and Queen? Surely Mr. Monroe couldn't have done it! Perhaps he made someone else do it to throw the suspicion far from him. If that was the case, who would he use for such a thing? The face of Miss Primpette surfaced in my mind. She was extremely fond of him, maybe more than I had supposed. This could provide motive. Then again, there were lots of women in the castle who were extremely fond of the Head Steward.

Another idea shot through my head, "Could it be one of the Ladies in Waiting?"

I thought of the flirtatious girls, Charlotte and Kelsey. They could be easily seduced into performing such a task for a dashing man.

Or perhaps it wasn't someone in the castle after all! It could be that Mr. Monroe actually had a wife who is forced to assist and cope with his dastardly schemes. Or he could have a partner in crime who's traveled around Europe with him. I recalled the shady conversation I had overheard in the dingy, creepy apartment of the alley.

I reached the servants entrance and began walking through the courtyard, ignoring the people around me as if they were only shadows in the wind. My mind pursued its quest for answers. He could have a daughter or a foreigner from another country. What if politics were involved? It could be that Mr. Monroe was actually in love with Princess Vanessa and is trying to get some money out of the deal. . . .most unlikely of course. Who (in their right mind) would fall in love with a girl like Princess Vanessa?! She was not of age to marry - yet. Next year she would turn fifteen, and then she would be free to be given in matrimony.

My head whirled with speculations and imaginations! The possibilities were endless. By this time I had just come upon the doorway leading into the east wing of the palace. As usual, I found Lin waiting for me inside.

"Hi Lin! How was the harp at Rose Steadfast's house?"

She seemed surprised at my happy salutation. "Um, it was good. Rose taught me a few new things and Roger lent me a music book. I know most of the notes but a few I had a hard time with. They said I can come over and play anytime I want."

"Well, that was very kind of them. See, Christian people are very nice," I said as we entered the grand hall.

Lin smiled, "Yeah, they are. In fact, I don't think I have met such nice people in a long time."

We entered the maid's dressing room and I slipped on my frilly deep blue uniform.

"So," Lin began as we were handed our list of chores from Miss Primpette, "did you make your decision?"

"Yes, I have."

"And?"

I waited to reply until we were out of Miss Primpette's hearing range. "I have decided to do the right thing, which is to tell the truth," I said in a low tone. I turned to Lin with uncertainty.

I caught her mouth just in time before she screamed out her horror and surprise. I pulled her out of the grand hall, into a study room and closed the door. When I was sure we were safe, I took my hand away from Lin's mouth.

"Are you crazy!!" she shouted.

I quickly put my hand back and she made strained, muffled sounds.

"You have to be quiet Lin! Or we'll be found out and both die!"

That silenced her immediately. I cautiously removed my hand for the second time.

Lin didn't say anything but a tear slipped down her cheek.

"Oh Lin!" I said feeling emotions rise in me, "please don't cry!"

"But I've never had a friend like you before Jacqueline. And now I'm going to lose you!"

I hardly knew how to respond, so I gave her a big hug and tried to swallow down my tears.

When I finally pulled away, I saw that Lin's cheeks were streaked with trails of tears.

"No one's ever been such a good friend to me before," Lin whispered.

"Lin, I am so happy to be your friend, but Jesus loves you and can be a better friend to you than me. I really wish you would accept Him."

Lin wiped her eyes. She looked straight at me with such a mixture of emotions that it was hard for me to read what she was feeling.

At that untimely moment, the door I had closed swung open and Lin and I found ourselves staring into the cynical face of. . . . . .Miss Hilda Primpette!

I backed away slowly and stuttered, "Miss Primpette! You scared us! I uh. . ."

"Miss Noble," the lady interrupted, her tone sharper than usual, "I have had quite enough of your nosy and disobedient ways. My patience has finally come to an end! I cannot stand seeing you neglect your work! Oh you might do your jobs well, I'll give you that. But I will not tolerate you spending even one minute of your work time in playful frivolity. It is simply unacceptable!"

I gulped at these reproofs. Even though Miss Primpette's tone was intimidating, her accusations did not consist of much foundation. Neglecting my work! The very idea! Just because she caught me in a room I wasn't assigned to be cleaning doesn't mean I was trying to get out of work! The prejudice of some people!

"Miss Primpette," I began in a voice that was almost pleading, "please don't think I would ever try to waste my time in useless frivolity. I. . ." I couldn't explain why I had taken shelter in this room because it would betray my secret!

However, it turned out I didn't have to explain at all, for Miss Primpette quickly replied, "The bottom line is I'm firing you."

I was taken aback, "What?!"

"Yes, you haven't passed the qualifications to be one of the Queen's maids. I will expect your uniform returned to Ms. Edna by the end of today. In the meantime, you will finish your morning responsibilities assigned for you and then receive your final payment. And as for you," the lady turned to Lin, "take this lesson and learn not to follow in the ways of such a girl."

"But Miss Primpette, please! I implore you!" I said clasping my hands together. "My brother needs the money I earn to go to school!"

"I'm terribly sorry my dear," she replied with a melancholy tone, "but once I have made a resolution, I stick to it. I'm sure you can find another job suited for your. . .station in life." And with that heart sinking statement, Miss Hilda Primpette closed the door.

For a moment, I had no idea where I was or what I was doing. I stood in a stunned daze for several minutes. Why! Why had this happened?! How *could* it happen?! I sank down to the floor in crushed defeat. What was I to do now? I covered my face with my hands.

"That devil woman," Lin murmured in hateful contempt.

I bit my lip hard to keep from crying.

I heard Lin kneel on the ground beside me. "It's going to be alright Jacqueline, you'll see. Perhaps its better you don't work here, with all the drama that's going on."

I shook my head despondingly. Slowly I slid my hands off of my face. "I *needed* this job. Mother believed in me so much - Phillip too. Why did I have to let them down?"

"You didn't let them down!" Lin said with earnest. "Miss Primpette just always caught you at the wrong place during the wrong time. She made a hasty, judgmental decision. You've done nothing to deserve it."

"Perhaps."

"No! You haven't," Lin confirmed again. Then her voice softened, "It'll be lonely working here without you."

I looked up at Lin's kind face and smiled with appreciation.

"That is, if the Miss Primpette lets me keep my job. I might have to slap her first," Lin added with a rueful grin.

This actually got a little laugh out of me. "If that's what your reaction is going to be, I can't wait to see what Carlos is going to do."

"Probably torch the palace," Lin replied casually as we both stood.

It felt good to have such loyal friends! I prayed with all my heart that Lin would someday come to repentance and faith.

"Does this instance change your decision about. . .you know what," Lin said as we made our way to the dining room to clean the floor.

I shook my head, "Unfortunately not."

Lin moaned, "Please! Act with some sense for once!"

"I'm sorry Lin but I won't go back on my decision."

"Carlos will be happy," my friend muttered under her breath.

"I'm not doing this for Carlos," I said. "I'm doing it because it's right."

Lin sniffed, "That's just your opinion."

I was actually getting pretty annoyed now, "Stop pestering me about it alright! My life's hard enough already."

Lin said no more. I could feel a cloak of tight tension fall on the room. We both cleaned fervently in the deafening silence. Neither of us spoke. To say that I didn't feel guilty about my reaction would certainly be a lie. I knew I shouldn't have snapped back, but, I just couldn't help it! No, that was wrong too, I *could* have helped it. After all, I'm the one who's a Christian. I should have acted more mature.

I heaved a sigh and began to apologize when another maid entered the room in a flurry. I recognized her as a young woman named Gina. She was the type of person who was anxious to please, but overly nervous of making a mistake. As she entered the dining room, it appeared she was in her usual tizzy.

"Oh what am I going to do?!" she moaned. In her distress the maid hadn't really noticed Lin and I.

I temporarily forgot my due apologies to Lin and asked, "What's the matter Gina?"

"Oh! I didn't know anyone was in here. Oh well. You'll never guess what I must do! It is perfectly burdensome!"

"Try me," I said dryly.

"Alright," Gina said with a smile - quite happy to be sharing her problems. "Queen Tabitha wants me to pick out a book of poems from her library and read it to her!"

I sighed, "Is that all?"

Quite annoyed by my lack of interest Gina went on, "Is that all!! I don't know what kind of poems Her Majesty enjoys! What if I got one she absolutely didn't like?! It would be perfectly terrible and embarrassing! I'm sure I could not bear to see Queen Tabitha disappointed!"

"Certainly not," I replied still scrubbing the glossy floor.

Gina put her hand on her forehead as if thinking, "The Queen requested poems that would cope with her mood. Well, I'd say I'd better get the most depressing poems I can find."

"Now hold on Gina," I said; an idea popping into my mind. "The Queen is already quite out of spirits. Shouldn't you try to brighten her day by getting happy poems?"

Gina looked frantic again, "Oh no! You're right! I should probably get happy poems! But Queen Tabitha did request sad poems. What am I going to do?!"

The poor girl looked like she was going to faint. I half grinned and walked up to her. "I will choose the poem if you like. And if the Queen doesn't like it, the heat will fall on me and not you. What do you say?"

"You'd do that, for me?! Oh thank you! I really should. . ."

"Don't mention it," I cut in quickly before she could have the chance to babble more.

Lin caught my eye before I left the dining room. From her expression I could tell she knew my plan, and was still displeased with me. When Gina had left the room I said, "I'm sorry Lin, for snapping back at you. Will you forgive me?"

Lin nodded mutely. She still didn't approve of my decision.

It was hard to be thought of as foolish by my friend.

I entered the Queen's library in a state of gloom. I looked over the books listlessly until my eyes alighted on a very peculiar name, Richard Lovelace. I knew he was a poet, but what a humiliating name for a man! I leafed through his book of poems until I found a really sad one called, Lucasta Weeping. Well, that was one that Queen Tabitha requested. Then I went looking for a more lighthearted one and came across Robert Herrick's poem To the Maids, To walk Abroad. I intended to read Herrick's poem instead of Lovelace's but, the Queen would have to make the decision herself.

I made my way up the white marble staircase and caught sight of Her Majesty sitting in the drawing room. I walked slowly and silently up to the door and watched as the poor Queen stared indolently out the window.

"She must feel terrible," I said to myself. I knocked on the door and the Queen turned around.

"Oh hello dear. Wait, you aren't the one I sent to read me a poem."

"No Your Majesty," I curtseyed, "but poor Gina didn't know what poem to read you so I offered to take the job for her."

"What a sweet girl you are," Queen Tabitha said with a soft smile. "I had requested a poem to cope with my mood."

"True my Queen. But wouldn't you want something a bit happier to lighten your low spirits?" I asked timidly.

Her Majesty considered a moment. I noticed that the Queen seemed lovelier when sober then when she was bubbly and rather absent minded. I truly felt very badly for her; the poor mother, losing her daughter in the most unsuspecting circumstance.

"Read the sorrowful poem first darling, and then you may read the other one."

I smiled and sat down on the sofa next to Her Majesty. You can imagine how important I felt, that I got to read a poem to the Queen of Lydonia herself!

I cleared my throat and Queen Tabitha resumed staring out the window.

"Lucasta Weeping, by Richard Lovelace.
Lucasta wept, and still the bright
Inamour'd God of Day.
But when her Teares his heatre or'e came,
In Clouds he quensht his Beames,
And griev'd, wept out his Eyes of Flame
So drowned her sad Streams." I paused here to take a breath. This really *was* depressing. I looked over at the Queen; she still held a dreamlike expression. How could someone enjoy this? Nevertheless, I read on. . .

"At this she smil'd when straight the Sun
Cheer'd, with her kindre desires;
And by her eyes Reflection,
Kindled againe his Fires."

I closed the book and looked at Her Majesty expectantly.

"That was pure poetry," she sighed. "Now I suppose you may read the lighthearted one."

"Queen Tabitha," I began quietly.

"Yes?"

"After the next poem, may I discuss something of importance with you?"

The Queen seemed not to notice the severity with which I asked her. "Yes of course," she replied.

I opened a book of poems by Robert Herrick. "To the Maids, To walk Abroad," I began.

"How appropriate," Her Majesty flashed me a small smile.

I grinned sheepishly and continued,
"Come, sit we under yonder tree,
Where merry maids we'll be;

And as on primroses we sit,
We'll venture if we can at wit;
If not, at draw gloves we will play,
So spend some minutes of the day;
Or else spin out the thread of sands,
Playing at questions and commands:
Or tell what strange tricks Love can do,
By quickly making one of two.
Thus we will. . ." I was interrupted by two young ladies entering the room. It was the Ladies in Waiting.

"Your Majesty," Charlotte began when she realized what was taking place, "surely you do not need a *maid* to read you poems. Such inconvenience! *I* shall do it! For I tell you I have the finest reading voice. . ."

"Beside me!" Kelsey put in; she was quite put out by her companion's boasting.

"Well, this young maid was doing just fine, don't you think?" Queen Tabitha replied.

"Oh, well, she might have been. But she is not one of your Ladies in Waiting, now is she?" Charlotte said giving me a spiteful glare.

Oh, I could have slapped her face! I looked at the Queen in desperation.

"I suppose your right Charlotte. She must get back to her duties. Thank you dear for reading to me. I feel much better now." Queen Tabitha gave me a kind smile and dismissed me with grace.

"But my Queen! There is something I have to tell you - without the present company," I added with a look at Charlotte.

"Surely you can tell me some other time?"

"No! This is urgent! It concerns. . ."

"You heard Her Highness! Do you dare disobey her? Get out," Kelsey commanded.

I looked at the faces around the room with pleading eyes. They *must* listen to me! But I had no chance, for the two Ladies in Waiting dragged me out of the room and shut the door in my face.

I stamped my foot in frustration! The self-centered people! They didn't deserve to know the truth! Why should I tell them?!

I stomped down the marble staircase in high indignation. I returned to the dining room and found that it had already been cleaned. I went to the next room and found Lin quietly dusting the grand piano forte.

Just as I stepped into the music room Lin looked up and her gaze met my eyes.

After a silent pause she asked, "So, did you tell the Queen?"

I sighed in disappointment and picked up my duster, "No."

Lin didn't reply for a while but continued to clean.

"They didn't give me a chance," I explained almost on the brink of tears. "I know it's the right thing to do, but I didn't know I had to fight in order to do it! I'm going to have to try again."

"How?" Lin asked.

"I'll find a way. . . .eventually."

Lin didn't say anything, but out of the corner of my eye I saw her shake her head in doubt.

"God," I prayed silently, "help!!"

I had to give the Queen the information before one o'clock so she could tell the king before it became too late.

I watched the clock anxiously from the corner of my eye all through my morning work schedule. Ten o'clock past. Eleven. Eleven-thirty.

At twelve o'clock my heart was literally racing! The Queen was hardly ever in sight and I couldn't leave to go find her because Miss Primpette was continually popping around in the most peculiar places; making sure I finished my assigned jobs.

The anxiety, the torturous anxiety! What was I going to do?! Lin hardly talked to me now because of reasons I'm sure you could guess, reader. It was painful to feel the rejection and disappointment of a friend. Twelve thirty is when all the maids take a break for lunch, but I couldn't wait till then! King Gilbert needed to know *now*! I kept praying for an opportunity.

The grand clock chimed twelve fifteen just as I stepped onto the lovely veranda. I took out my sweeper and began to brush back and forth the leaves that had collected in the corners and cracks of the graceful porch. And then, from somewhere in the garden, I heard someone whistling. I brushed a long hair curl that dangled in my face and looked around. My eyes brightened a little as I recognized Carlos walking towards the veranda.

"Hey Carlos!" I greeted with a wave.

"Buenos Dias Jacqueline!" he hailed back.

He came up the veranda's steps and sat on the railing.

I could barely contain myself any longer, "You'll never guess what I have decided to do!"

"What?" he prodded with a smile.

"You will be pleased to know that I am going to reveal all that I know concerning. . . you know what, to the King and Queen!"

It gave me great satisfaction to see his dark eyes light up and his face split into an approving grin.

"That is awesome!! I knew you'd do the right thing! I'm so proud of you!" he exclaimed leaping up from his seat.

"Well, it's sure nice to get some encouragement," I remarked with a wan smile.

Carlos frowned, "Lin?"

I nodded.

He waved his hands, "Forget about her! *You're* doing what's right and that's all that matters. I never really could agree with that Asian girl anyways."

"Carlos! Shame on you," I scolded. "She is just doing what she thinks will keep me safe! Remember, just because you happen to be right this time doesn't mean you'll be right every time."

"True enough," he said raising his hands in surrender; but his smile told me he thought there would be little chance of him *ever* being wrong.

"So," Carlos began, "when are you going to tell. . ."

But he was interrupted by someone stepping onto the veranda.

Both our heads turned and I was dumbstruck with surprise at seeing Queen Tabitha.

"And she's alone!" I thought with glee.

This was my moment, I just knew it! I nearly pushed poor Carlos off the railing trying to make him scarce. Thankfully, he got the idea and immediately vanished.

The Queen smiled at me and took a seat on one of the tea table chairs.

"A beau of yours?" she asked with a twinkle in her eye.

I waved my hand carelessly at the absurd assumption, "No, Carlos is just a friend."

"Of course," the queen replied with a smile.

Ugh! Grown-ups. They have the weirdest ideas. "You're Highness, may I discuss the important issue I mentioned earlier to you?"

"Yes of course," Queen Tabitha replied, still unaffected by my serious tone.

I seated myself on a chair beside her; my hands getting sweaty and my stomach filled with butterflies. "Well," I began rather unsteadily, "I have some information that I think will interest you."

And so, I told my story.

Chapter Eleven

Tests of the Heart

*Q*ueen Tabitha sat in her plush chair on the beautiful palace veranda in overwhelmed shock and confusion.

"Do you mean to say, child," she began after a deathly silence, "that Jacob Monroe, the Head Steward, is responsible for this catastrophe?"

I nodded in sober silence.

Queen Tabitha placed her hand on her forehead, looking as if she was about to faint from all the information I had given her. "Can it be true," she said talking to herself. The Queen looked at me. "Or are you lying? What am I to believe?!" she stated in exasperation.

"You must believe me Your Highness!" I said going on my knees. "I know I may not look like much, but I *do* know the truth! And if you do not listen to me, King Gilbert will be giving a ludicrous amount of money to a traitor that works at his own home!"

Queen Tabitha seemed to recognize the outrage of the situation and stood to her feet in firm resolution, "Lying or not, your story must be told to the King. If it is true, we might be able to save this country and my daughter from hurt and embarrassment. This tragic issue should have never taken place! I am still surprised that it happened. Come, Jacqueline Noble, I will take you to Gilbert, and you will share with him this story of yours."

My eyes glowed from her words and my stomach turned in knots in mixed excitement and fear. I hoped Mr. Monroe didn't catch and kill me before going in front of the King.

Queen Tabitha summoned her Ladies in Waiting and ordered them to make me presentable to go before King Gilbert.

I smiled at the irony. Charlotte and Kelsey turned red in the face at the command. But they followed through just as the Queen had told them. My hot, dewy face was wiped with a cool white towel and my hair was brushed to perfection and placed in a bun that allowed a few of my curls to cascade down gracefully onto my neck. My maid's outfit was straightened and my mob cap frilled up so that it looked brand new!

As I looked in the mirror, I was struck with the contrast of my outward tidiness and my inward turmoil. My heart fluttered with hope and anxiety at a rate that was hard to calculate. I was going before the *King*. The King of Lydonia! My mind tried to grasp that reality! Imagine, reader, going in front of the leader of your country! I was too preoccupied with this that I didn't really notice the cold disdainful faces of the Ladies in Waiting.

I came out of the Queen's dressing room looking nice yet sick to my stomach.

"Excellent! Follow me," Queen Tabitha directed.

I walked through the grand hall; a feeling of importance swelling in my breast such as I had never felt before! Imagine being escorted by the Queen of Lydonia!!

I had a fiendish delight watching all the maids stare at me in awe as I passed by with the Queen. However, my smile faded when my eyes met Lin's stare.

My friend's eyes were sad and full of fear. I saw Lin bite her lip to keep from crying.

Oh how my heart went out to her! If she only understood! Our gaze did not last very long for soon I was out of the east wing and striding through the center of the castle.

I walked past beautiful paintings, furniture, statues, pillars, staircases, tapestries, grand windows, draping curtains, servants, maids, butlers, and all the regal elements of the palace. We journeyed to a part of the castle I had never been to. It was the area leading to the north wing; which is where the King's quarters.

We stopped in front of a golden door marked North Wing. Two strong, robustly built guards protected the entranceway. When they saw the Queen, the guards immediately separated their long ancient spears and let Her Majesty through. Kelsey opened the golden door while Charlotte exchanged a flirtatious glance with one of the guards.

When we entered the north wing, I could tell it gave off a different feel than the east or west wing. It was more regal and stately than any other part of the castle. It was less graceful and flowery. From the deep red flowing curtains to the golden gilt chandeliers, everything spoke of royal authority.

A smartly dressed butler with a suave British accent and slick black hair painted with grey welcomed us.

"My dear Queen," he said smiling beneath his thin black mustache while giving a professional bow.

"Good morning Mr. Bridges. Is Gilbert available?" the Queen asked.

"He is in a meeting with Detective Martin madam."

"Good, tell him I must see him."

"Of course," the butler said making a slight bow.

I twirled my fingers around in nervous agitation. Would King Gilbert believe me? I hoped so.

Queen Tabitha must have noticed my uneasiness for she started talking about other things to make me feel more comfortable.

"That butler who just assisted us is Mr. Barry Bridges. He has been my husband's personal butler for twelve years. He moved to Lydonia from England when he was just a lad of sixteen. Mr. Bridges came to work for us when he was thirty six. You have a slight French accent Jacqueline. Did you live in France for a while before coming to this country?"

I nodded, "Yes, You're Majesty. My family moved from France to Lydonia when I was eleven."

"Ah," the Queen said with a nod, "in 1776 right? Yes, I remember that year. King Gilbert and I heard of some sort of revolution in the American colonies. The people wanted to break away from England I understand. Mr. Bridges was quite upset about it, since it was his home country. As for me, I say good for them! I wish the colonies well."

I smiled. So, the Queen did have a political opinion.

"How old are you my dear?" the Queen asked.

"Thirteen," I replied.

The Queen seemed a bit surprised and so were the Ladies in Waiting.

"You're thirteen, and you're willing to go before the King! Bravo," Kelsey exclaimed with a smile that conveyed admiration.

Charlotte sighed in exasperation and rolled her eyes in obvious indifference.

A few moments later the butler, Mr. Bridges, returned. The knot in my stomach came with him and a lump in my throat formed.

"The King is ready to see you now my Queen," Mr. Bridges informed pleasantly.

"Very good," Queen Tabitha replied as she swept passed.

Our little group strode down a hall that had a rich velvet red carpet leading up to a gorgeous deep cherry wood door. Two overhanging curtains lined with beautiful tassels draped across the large doorway. Charlotte took hold of the curving, golden gilt handle and swung the door wide open.

My heart was beating so hard I was afraid the others would hear it!

As the door was opened a flood of light entered the hall and made me squint for a moment. When my eyes adjusted I was ushered by the Queen into an enormous library. This large room was adorned with beautiful, enormous glass windows. The sunshine poured in and illuminated every corner, making the whole atmosphere warm and inviting. My eyes wandered to some of the titles on the glossy wooden bookshelves. For a moment I was diverted as I recognized many famous authors. But this little glimmer of imagination lasted for a second. I soon became aware that I was approaching a grand desk. A square shouldered man with penetrating eyes sat behind it. It was the King.

My pace slowed and my hands started to quiver a bit. He looked so wise, so regal, strong in will and authority. I felt small and intimidated with awe as I approached the desk with the Queen. Another man of smaller height with a long face stood next to His Majesty. I was guessing he was Detective Martin.

The King rose to greet his wife, but I could tell it was mixed with sadness.

Queen Tabitha must have noticed it for she immediately exclaimed, "No good news?"

King Gilbert shook his head, "I'm afraid not. I have just been talking with Detective Martin and he says this case is difficult."

"Well, I may be able to shed some light on this thick fog. That is, if this young lady's story is true," Her Majesty said with a glance at me.

King Gilbert and Detective Martin focused their attention immediately on me. I looked up into their faces for as long as I could until I finally dropped my gaze.

"You say this young girl knows something of the whereabouts of our daughter?" the king prodded his eyes shifting to the Queen.

"Yes darling, and if you will just hear her out, I'm sure you will find the information interesting."

"Very well," His Majesty nodded taking a seat that was near me. He offered me the chair next to him and then waited for me to speak.

I sat down with a quiver. All three people's eyes were staring expectantly at me. I found it hard to articulate my words correctly - but I would do this, I was determined!

"You have nothing to fear my dear, tell me everything you know," the King's kind, deep voice assured me.

"Well, Your Majesty," I began, "this might be hard to believe, but the criminal you are seeking is a worker of your own palace."

I saw a spark of indignation flare up in the king's piercing eyes, "Go on."

And so, I went on to tell the entire story from start to finish. No one interrupted me until I ended with, "And so you see sir, I would have told you before, but my life and my family's lives were threatened. Only now do I have the courage to tell the truth, please believe me."

King Gilbert's face went from attentive to studious. He sat back in his chair and sank into deep thought.

Detective Martin was the first to speak, "Well, you were right my Queen, that *was* an interesting story. Probably one she *made* up!"

The Queen looked sharply at the detective, "Do you really think so? I thought it was pretty reliable. I mean, the maids see everything we don't."

"Perhaps they do, but honestly, why would they report it to you?! If the story is true, which I highly doubt, then how could a girl of *thirteen* undergo so much life-threatening pressure and still have the courage to tell the truth. I say it is simply against the natural inclination. It's preposterous!" Mr. Martin's narrow eyes glared at me. He appeared very, very angry and annoyed.

I caught myself staring at the detective with interest. That voice, it sounded strangely familiar.

I looked over at the King and saw he was still pondering what to do.

With my disposition readers, you can imagine the heated feelings that boiled up inside me against Detective Martin. How could he!

Then it dawned on me. . .that voice! I turned sharply to Detective Martin and instantly knew he must have been the Mr. Martin Jacob Monroe had talked to in that apartment!

I could hardly stand it! My only hope was that the King would somehow take heed to my story and stop Jacob Monroe and this rotten detective! My mind froze at the idea of being strangled by Mr. Monroe. No, I had come too far. . .I was not going to lose this battle!

"You're Highness, please!" I begged going on my knees. "You must believe me! You mustn't listen to this corrupt detective – he's in it too! I heard him speaking to Jacob Monroe. . ."

"Your Majesty, this evil little girl has cost us enough time and trouble! Listen no more to her heinous lies!"

The King rose, but I persisted in my protests. . .

"Your Highness please listen! A large amount of money and the lives of my family and I depend on it!"

Mr. Martin countered, "You're Majesty it is impossible! This girl is accusing a man of the crime, and yet, the ransom note was written by a woman. It doesn't connect!!"

"Please!" I said my eyes starting to fill with tears.

"Your Majesty this girl is playing a trick on you! She's probably an accomplice to the real kidnapper! She's leading you on the wrong track! Throw her out, I implore you."

The King closed his eyes and with a firm deep voice replied, "Cease!"

Mr. Martin immediately shut up. The room went silent. After a long pause King Gilbert resumed speaking, "This is a very hard decision, but I must make it. Young lady, thank you for telling me your story, I will take it into consideration; but for now, I will be faithful to the plans Detective Martin has laid out. Good day to you Miss. . ."

"Jacqueline Noble," I replied in a very weak, almost inaudible voice.

"Jacqueline Noble," the King finished quietly as he reseated himself on the chair behind the large desk.

The world went blank to me. Could this really have happened?! I wanted to run from the room and burst out crying, but my limbs were too numb to even move. I became aware that Queen Tabitha was gently ushering me out of the library. I couldn't bear to look into the faces of the Ladies in Waiting or the butler Barry Bridges. I was escorted out of the north wing door.

Before I continued to the east wing the Queen stopped me.

"I'm so sorry dear. I thought perhaps. . .well, anyways, some things aren't meant to work out."

I couldn't resist a heavy tear as it fell down my cheek. Before the Queen could register more heartfelt affection I turned my heel and quickly left.

No caresses could cure the struggling feelings inside me. I had lost everything in one day, my mission, my job, and who knows, my life might end pretty soon as well. There was no way I could face Lin again. She would think I was a failure. What kind of testimony was that?! I wiped away a stream of tears from my hot face as I made my way to the maid's dressing room. Miss Primpette had instructed me to return my uniform and give it to Edna at the end of my morning chores.

I shut the door and slowly let the maid dress fall from my shoulders. I felt as if I had been stripped of all happiness. My family was probably going to have to move in order to avoid being butchered by Mr. Monroe. Another move, oh that sounded horrible! I put on my homemade dress and slung my brown bag over my shoulder. I wandered into the grand hall and searched for Edna.

"Where are you Edna," I mumbled in frustration after searching most of the rooms. She had to be around here somewhere. Suddenly my eyes fell on a mirror. I stared at my reflection. Was I really all alone in this?

A small still voice inside me whispered, "I will never leave you or forsake you."

Another tear made its way down my cheek. No, I was not alone. God was with me. I had done the right thing, and He knows I am not a failure. Thank goodness He loves me more than I could ever love myself. Surely Jesus knows how to take care of me better than anyone.

Right then and there I knelt on my knees and thanked God for giving me the grace to accomplish what was right and good. I surrendered myself to his will once again, forcing myself to believe He knew best.

"I don't understand! Why did you let this happen to me?" I whispered to Him.

I bit my lip. This was extremely hard! I couldn't see how anything good could come out of this! But when I stood up from that prayer, I miraculously felt better.

"Well Jacqueline Noble," I said to myself in the mirror, "looks like you're going to be starting another adventure."

And so, I slung my bag over my shoulder and walked out of the room straight into the face of. . . . . .Edna.

"Edna! Hi! I was just looking for you. I. . ."

"Yes, I know. Miss Primpette told me to find you. Here is your final pay and a slip of paper saying you have finished your job and accept the money we paid you. Sign here," she pointed to the bottom of the page.

I took the money and placed it carefully in my bag. Taking the quill pen I sat down and began to sign my name.

Suddenly I stopped. My eyes looked over the paper's writings. A flash of realization took hold of me!!

"Edna?" I asked.

The elderly maid sighed, "What?"

"Who wrote up this sheet of paper?"

"I did. Why?"

My heart started beating faster. The handwriting was the exact same as the ransom note!!

I tried to conceal my surprise and excitement. "Oh nothing, I was just curious."

I handed the slip of paper back to Edna and then exited the room. There was nothing I could do about it now. My theories were not accepted. With a firm nod of my head I decided to not get involved anymore. But that couldn't keep my mind from wandering to the startling facts that were now becoming clear to me.

My footsteps echoed on the floor of the servant's court-yard as I walked through. I nodded my head in courtesy to the guards and then started on the road leading to Lyden.

The afternoon sun shown brilliantly over the busy town. A light breeze wafted across the landscape. I closed my eyes and breathed in the refreshing air. I suddenly had the impulse to let my hair down. How soothing it would be to let down the tight bun from my head. With a tug I loosed my bun and let my soft brown, wavy curls fall onto my back. Ah, relief! For some strange reason, in the midst of all that was happening, I felt peaceful. Yes, God would protect those who did his will - I was counting on it.

Chapter Twelve

The Moment of Truth

So, to pick up where I left off, I was heading into the town of Lyden.

Now, considering what I just went through, I was doing pretty good. It's amazing to think how God helped me through all that.

I was just about to enter the town, reciting what I was going to say to Mother when I heard my name being called. Somewhat surprised I looked up and searched for a familiar face in the crowd. Then it came again, "Jacqueline! Miss Noble!!"

"Who in the world could that be?" I asked myself. Finally I turned around and beheld a teenage girl running towards me. I squinted and in surprise exclaimed, "Kelsey? Is that you!"

"Yes," she said coming up to me and panting. After a few moments of deep breathing she continued, "You have to come back to the castle."

"Why?"

"Because! Queen Tabitha and King Gilbert want to see you," she replied still trying to catch her breath.

"I don't understand. I though they didn't. . ."

"Do me a favor," she said placing her hand on my shoulder, "don't think! Just come! They need to talk to you now and I am not returning without you!"

"Alright! Don't get all flustered up, I'll come," I said in an effort to calm the girl.

We both ran back to the castle in haste. My mind was racing nearly as fast as my feet. Why did the royal family want to see me again? It didn't make sense unless. . .perhaps.

We flashed past the servant's courtyard and the maids. Everything was in a whirl until we were stopped by Miss Primpette in the central area of the castle.

"And just where do you girls think your going? Especially you!" she said pointing her sharp finger at me.

"If you would please move, I might be able to accomplish what the King and Queen have assigned me to do! Now make way!" Kelsey said in a huff as she took hold of my hand and ran past the fuming Head Supervisor.

I gulped. I wondered if we should have crossed Miss Primpette in that way. We were bound to pay for it. I looked behind me. With horror I saw Miss Primpette charging after us.

"She's following us!" I said to Kelsey as we entered the north wing.

"Nonsense! She can't do anything to us," Kelsey exclaimed with a toss of her head.

We were allowed in by the King's personal guards and then led to the library by Mr. Bridges. I felt much more confident than my first arrival; though my mind was still in a puzzle of confusion. Why was I here again? What did they want?

When I entered the library, I noted that Detective Martin was nowhere in sight. The only people that stood there was King Gilbert, Queen Tabitha, and the Lady in Waiting, Charlotte.

"Here you are Your Majesties. This is the very same girl you talked with earlier," Kelsey said with a curtsey.

I curtseyed as well and made sure it was the most elegant I had ever done.

"Miss Noble, right?" King Gilbert asked.

"Yes Your Highness," I replied meekly.

"Well, I'm glad to have found you. You are probably wondering why you sent for again."

"Yes sir."

"Well, it just so happens that after hearing your story, I decided to double check Detective Martin's credentials and. . ." he paused.

Queen Tabitha finished, "We found a sort of glitch in his papers."

"This slight problem has annoyed me with doubt and I have taken Mr. Martin into custody. Since time is running out and we have no other alternative, the Queen and I have decided to believe your story and act upon it. We must make a plan of attack."

I blinked several times, "Really?"

"Really," the Queen replied with a smile.

I could have cried with joy but instead I simply said, "Thank you, thank you, thank you Your Majesties."

The King waved my gratitude aside hastily, "I need your help. I have assembled a group of my finest soldiers to arrest this Jacob Monroe. I want you to show them where this villain is keeping my daughter. When you have recovered Vanessa, it will be perfectly clear that you were right. But if you do not, I'm afraid the results will be devastating. Are we clear on that?"

"Quite my King," I said with a tremble of excitement.

His Majesty nodded firmly and then turned to his desk and rang a bell. Mr. Bridges arrived promptly and bowed deeply to his master.

"Yes sir?"

"Barry, summon Keith Stone immediately and tell him to bring four men with him."

"Yes my lord." Mr. Bridges bowed again then exited.

I glowed with excitement and goose-bumps! Everything was going to work out! We *would* catch this villainous man after all!

"And his accomplices," I murmured tilting my eyebrow. It still puzzled me how Edna could somehow be entangled in this crime - but I was sure it wouldn't be long before I found out!

Don't get me wrong reader, I knew there was still danger ahead, but the knowledge that the King and Queen heeded my information, encouraged me.

I clasped my hands behind my back in agitation as we all waited for Mr. Stone. My eyes roved over the room until they rested on a beautiful clock. The time Mr. Monroe was to receive the bag of money was one thirty. The clock read one o'clock. I bit my lip. We had to get going! He couldn't slip through our fingers!

At that moment Mr. Barry Bridges walked into the room again, this time accompanied by Mr. Keith Stone.

Keith Stone was a very tall, muscular man with dirty blond hair and a striking face. From his attire it was obvious he served the King as Captain of the Royal Guards.

Captain Stone saluted gallantly, "You summoned me, my lord."

"Yes Captain. It appears that this young lady here knows the location of where Princess Vanessa is being held captive. She also knows the perpetrator who committed this crime. We will try to catch him before he gets the chance to escape."

Captain Stone's clear green eyes glinted with a surge of energy and excitement, "And who is this villain my King?"

"I believe his name is Jacob Monroe, the Head Steward of the castle."

I turned to look at Keith Stone and saw a spark of anger flash in his eye.

"I understand that Mr. Monroe's lair is somewhere in the town of Lyden. If your men dress in formal uniform, it would cause commotion in the streets and alert the kidnapper of their arrival. I propose you go dressed as mere townsfolk until you have rescued my daughter and secure the criminal."

"It shall be done as you wish my King," Captain Stone replied with a bow and then turned to leave the room.

"Ah Captain," King Gilbert said motioning him to stay, "aren't you forgetting something?"

"Am I?"

Both the King and the Queen pointed to me. I felt so shy and nervous.

"This is Miss Jacqueline Noble, and she will lead you to the criminal and the Princess. Remember, this entire affair has been quite hidden from the general public, and I want to keep it that way."

"Of course," Captain Stone replied with a nod.

I walked over to Captain Stone and we began to take our leave.

We strode out of the library and into the King's greeting hall where four strong young men stood at attention. When they saw me, I noticed puzzled looks cross their faces.

"Gentleman," Captain Keith Stone began, "this assignment will hopefully end this ridiculous incident of the Princess's kidnap. King Gilbert has given me the intelligence that the criminal is the Head Steward, Jacob Monroe. He is holding Princess Vanessa somewhere in our town of Lyden. I have been instructed to suit you men in clothes common to the townspeople. This young lady here is going to guide us to where this villainous snake is hiding the king's daughter. Do you understand?"

"Yes sir," they all said at once.

Immediately they left to change into their town costumes. I had never witnessed a captain commanding his men before and thought it was quite interesting.

"It must be somewhat enjoyable to watch these men do whatever you tell them," I remarked to the captain as we stood there waiting.

I looked up at him and to my disappointment it seemed as if he wouldn't respond. It wasn't until I sighed that he replied, "Somewhat."

The four guards were back and we set out for the town.

We marched through the palace and out the servant's courtyard (we used this entranceway because it would be less conspicuous) and out onto the road leading to the town.

I knew time was quickly slipping through our grasp and I kept up a hurried pace as we entered Lyden. The tall buildings blotted out the warm sun as we entered the backstreets.

As we neared the alley where I had been threatened by Mr. Monroe, the guards fell behind and relied on my direction. I won't lie, it was pretty awesome having these men following *my* lead!

Anyway, back to the real situation. The crowds began to disperse as we came closer and closer to the darker alleys. I was racking my brain for something that would call to memory the exact alley.

"Miss ah. . .what was your name again?" Captain Stone asked after we had walked a while.

"Jacqueline."

"Jacqueline, are you sure you know where this place is?"

"Of course," I said in a tone that betrayed my uncertainty.

Keith Stone gave me a skeptical look, "You do not sound very sure of yourself."

"I am. It just takes some time trying to single out the exact alley out of all these."

"We don't have time for searching!" one guard expressed urgently.

"Stay your ground Steven, and hide that gun beneath your cloak! We will do as the King commanded."

"They are getting restless," I told myself. "I need to find that alley - fast!"

The tension was mounting in my chest, for the clock in the town square had just given a big dong sound as it struck one thirty!

What if Jacob Monroe had found out the King had sent his guards?! What if he had escaped?! Or, he could be waiting in Stallion Meadow for his bag of cash. Either way it was not a good thing!

I started running, looking into every alley, trying to remember which one it was!

Sweat started to trickle down my forehead as my eyes darted from one place to another.

We *had* to be near it now!

I took sharp intakes of breath as my heart beat faster, faster, faster. . .

I ran and ran until. . .

I skidded to a stop and the men behind me nearly all collided together.

I walked back a few paces.

My pulse racing, I entered the alley cautiously. A funnel of chilly wind swept through the narrow street, blowing my hair in swirls all around my sweaty face. I folded my arms together to keep warm and continued to proceed. Filthy rubbish littered the sides of the cobblestone ground.

The royal guards followed me through the shadows. I turned to make sure they were close behind. There was no way I was advancing through this place alone. A sliver of light made Captain's Stone's gun glint before it once again vanished beneath the folds of his deep cloak.

I came upon a door which led into the building that covered the left side of the alley.

A cold shiver went through my body as I remembered how my throat had been held tightly against that door.

"Is this it?" Captain Stone asked above a whisper.

I nodded.

"We'll take it from here Jacqueline. . ."

The words were barely out of the captain's mouth when a gunshot whistled through the air and a zip of wind was felt on the side of my head.

"Take cover!" Captain Stone commanded as he lowered my head and then covered me protectively with his cape.

I didn't dare look up. My head pounded and ears rattled with the sound of several gunshots. And then, a cry from down the alley was heard just as someone fired. After that, everything became silent.

I could hear my heart thudding in my chest.

"I think I got him Captain!" came the triumphant voice of one of the guards.

"So you did Matthew, so you did!" Captain Stone confirmed; satisfaction evident in his tone. "Well done!"

My head was uncovered and my eyes eagerly surveyed the situation. Everything looked as it had before.

"What happened?" I asked.

Captain Stone pointed to the door.

I observed that a bullet had dented its surface.

"Mr. Monroe shot at you from the opposite end of the alley. It nearly missed your head."

I looked at the dented door and then back at the captain with enlarged eyes.

He smiled, "It would seem Someone is watching out for you."

I gulped and then returned his smile.

"Everything should go much more smoothly from here," Keith Stone replied replacing his pistol, "we've injured the kidnapper and have him in custody."

"But what about the money the King was supposed to give Mr. Monroe?" I asked.

"What do you mean?"

"Well, I thought Mr. Monroe was going to pick it up – and yet he is here and the clock has already struck 1:30 p.m.! Shouldn't he be in the Stallion's Meadow and not here?"

The Captain nodded dismissively, "No doubt he sent an accomplice to finish that job. I have men posted near the spot – the accomplice will not escape."

For the first time, I felt myself sigh with relief.

"And now, Jacqueline," Captain Stone stated turning to me, "where is the Princess?"

I directed Captain Stone to the eerie basement where I had caught a glimpse of Princess Vanessa that dreadful day.

To my utter relief, we found that Her Highness was still there!

A group of royal, gallant guards rushed to untie Her Majesty's bonds and free her from discomfort and fear.

Thankfully, Princess Vanessa was not seriously injured, just a little bruised, cranky, and tired. She was truly grateful to be rescued from this "hideous abode" as she put it.

However, once the Princess caught sight of me, her demeanor changed to one of utter shock. "What! What are you doing here Jack Maid?" she cried.

"Actually Your Highness, this girl is the heroine of the day. She is the one who led us to you, and your kidnapper," Captain Stone replied with an approving smile at me. He bent down to untie Her Majesty's hands.

Princess Vanessa looked at me narrowly, as if wondering to herself how a little, poor maid like me to do something like that.

I gave her a confident smile.

She sniffed, "Well it's not like it was hard to find me! I was right here under everyone's noses for goodness sake! Anyone with half a mind would have found me if they just took the time to look!" she turned her gaze to Captain Stone and gave him a glare of impatience.

I looked at her in disgust.

The guards knew better than to contradict her comments, so each bit his tongue and waited to follow their Captain's command.

The Captain stared down icily at the pretty, young Princess. "Perhaps you would have preferred to stay here Your Highness?" he offered.

"Don't mock me!" she replied erecting herself. "I have endured things no royal should this past week and I will not be talked to in that tone!"

"Then you will kindly follow me," the Captain replied in a strong voice that instantly subdued her.

Mr. Monroe was dragged back to the palace for questioning while Princess Vanessa was restored to her family and home.

I shared with the Captain of the Royal Guards my theory that the maid Edna was somehow connected with the crime. He immediately had the elderly lady sent for and taken to the questioning room.

While the criminal and his accomplices were being interrogated by the King, Queen Tabitha had taken me aside and began treating me like royalty. She was deeply grateful to me for recovering her precious, beautiful daughter from that 'traitorous, terrible man'.

I was sincerely happy to have done the royal family and Lydonia a great service. It pleased me to see the Queen joyful and back to her natural, exuberant self! Princess Vanessa was also very grateful to be home again, though she would never admit it in my presence. Even the Ladies in Waiting treated me with a little more respect.

I just sat in a hazy state of extreme relief and contentment!

"I cannot thank you enough for what you have done dear," the Queen cooed as she watched the Ladies in Waiting brush another stroke of my hair for the hundredth time.

"Thank you Your Highness!" I said with a wan smile. "It's a good thing God helped me or there is no way I could have done such a thing."

"Oh Jacqueline, you have such a sweet disposition," Queen Tabitha complimented. Then she turned to her daughter, "Doesn't she Vanessa?"

"Of course," her daughter stated sarcastically.

"And to think you almost got shot with a bullet!" Kelsey exclaimed with admiring eyes.

"It must have been scary and rather dreadful," Charlotte added with an evasive grin.

My mind began to go over what I had just been through. I couldn't wait to share my story with Lin and Carlos! It would be such fun to see their faces! I nearly giggled at the thought. Mother and Phillip would certainly be relieved to hear everything was done and laid at rest.

At that moment, I looked up to see a tall lady bustle into the room. "You're Majesty!" Miss Primpette exclaimed when she saw me sitting in the vanity chair in front of a gold mirror.

"I demand an explanation of what is going on! Earlier today I caught this young maid running through the castle like a maniac with your Lady in Waiting, Miss Barnes! What is the meaning of all this?"

I bit my lip and turned to see the Queen's response.

Queen Tabitha dismissed Miss Primpette's sharp tone with a wave of her hand, "My dear lady, you are troubling yourself over something quite unimportant."

"But I must know - ah, Your Majesty," the Head Supervisor stated trying to maintain a steady, respectful tone.

What is it of your concern?" the Queen said; still unwilling to share the events because of the king's wish to keep the matter quiet.

"If you must be told Your Highness, this girl was fired from her duty as one of your maids this morning. I would like to know why she is still here, operating wildly and freely," Miss Primpette said giving me narrow look.

The Queen seemed surprised, "You fired her! Under what cause?!"

"Neglecting work," the lady replied with superiority.

"I cannot believe that such a devoted child could commit such a thing," Her Majesty stated. "Let me tell you what she has just done. . ."

And the Queen informed Miss Primpette of my recent adventure.

I watched with satisfaction as Miss Primpette stood there, shock written all over her face!

When Queen Tabitha ended the story, Miss Primpette could just stutter words, "I..I never thought that. . .well, such a thing could take place and a girl no more than thirteen. . ."

There was a pause.

Finally, Miss Primpette cleared her throat, "I appear to have underestimated you, Miss Noble. You have proven your loyalty to the Queen quite efficiently. You can under-stand however, I merely judged from the little I saw so. . ."

I smiled, "All's well that ends well Madame Primpette."

I could see the lady was pleased with my gracious reply, "There's a good girl. I. . ."

But she couldn't finish, for Captain Keith Stone entered the room and reported, "King Gilbert wishes to see Her Majesty, Queen Tabitha, and Miss Jacqueline Noble."

I quickly stood up from my chair and followed the Queen out the door.

We entered a small, elegant room where Mr. Jacob Monroe sat in the center on a chair; his hands stiffly tied to his back.

King Gilbert offered two chairs to the Queen and me and then introduced the criminal.

I could see the hatred and rage in the eyes of the Head Steward when our eyes met. He seemed to be screaming, "You little traitorous wretch! I let you live and yet you betrayed me!"

But I wasn't the one in the hot seat now, he was. This gave me some confidence to stare back at him.

"Mr. Monroe," the King began, "you are guilty of treason against the Royal Crown of Lydonia. You kidnapped the rightful heir to the throne, my daughter, Princess Vanessa. I would now like you to share with my wife, and this young girl, the sinful details of how you did this."

Captain Stone entered the room at this point and gave Mr. Monroe a hard look and stated, "Obey the His Majesty's command."

Here it was, the moment of truth. Everything was to be revealed. Mr. Monroe couldn't escape it!

After a few silent, intense minutes, the villain gave in, "It started two years ago. I had run into some trouble in the town of Sailport, near the coast of Lydonia. I owed some rascals down there money, and couldn't pay for it. They wanted my blood. I escaped the town during the night and made my way to Lyden. I thought that at least in a city so far away, they wouldn't look for me. I had experience working as a butler for Earl Hemsworth and decided to try for a job as the Head Steward for the castle. I got it, and finally thought my troubles were over. Then one day, one of the men from Sailport found me. I never saw him, but he sent a man called Henry Martin to me with continual threats."

Here Captain Stone stepped in and added, "We discovered that Henry Martin is a corrupt officer of our town department that has given in to at least six shady bribes this year."

The King nodded and then motioned for Mr. Monroe to continue.

"You must understand," the man began with some emotion, "I have never been rich or given a chance to be wealthy in all my life! So I found that I didn't have the heart to pay this vile blackmailer out of my heavy salary, and there was no way I was running again, so, I devised a plan. The idea to kidnap Princess Vanessa seemed like a way to get the money I owed, and leave me with some extra cash. So, with the help of my mother, who traveled with me, I kidnapped Her Highness the night of the ball. You know the rest."

"Who is the accomplice you sent to pick up the King's money?" Captain Stone asked.

Mr. Monroe sighed, "My mother."

"Who is your mother?"

Mr. Monroe lifted his head and gave the Captain a sharp look. He didn't reply.

"Edna," I said more to myself than to the group.

"What was that dear?" the Queen asked.

"The maid Edna," I said a bit louder, "the one who also wrote the ransom note – right?"

"Yes. My mother has helped through the years with all my troubles. She was happy to assist me in this instance."

The room became quiet for a few seconds and then the King stood, "Well, this has all been cleaned up and solved very nicely. Good work Captain."

"Thank you sir."

"And the same to you young lady," His Majesty expressed turning to me.

I could feel myself glow with pride.

After the questions had been answered, Captain Stone took Mr. Monroe away to carry out the lawful punishment for his crime. Then, Edna Monroe was called and sentenced to prison for assisting her son in his treason.

By this time, evening was slowly settling over the land.

When each criminal had been given his due consequence, King Gilbert pulled me aside.

"I cannot say how proud I am of you, my young maid. You have shown wit and bravery today that is truly beautiful and rare. I would gladly honor you publicly, but as you know, this affair had to be kept quiet. And so, my dear girl, I can merely present you with this medal of courage, and my deepest thanks."

My heart swelled with joy and appreciation. I said a little prayer to myself, "Thank you Jesus, for helping me through this hard situation! It was worth it!"

"Thank you my King," I replied with a deep curtsey. My eyes sparkled as the King of Lydonia himself pinned a beautiful lilac shaped medal onto my dress.

"Now, if there is anything you wish for, please do not hesitate to ask," he said with a warm smile.

"Well actually Your Highness, there is one thing."

"Yes?"

"May I please have my job back as one of the Queen's maids?"

King Gilbert seemed a bit surprised by my request, "Really? Is that all? Wouldn't you rather be one of my daughter's Ladies in Waiting? It is a higher position and your daring rescue and loyalty to the crown I'm sure has impressed her."

I winced at the thought of being Princess Vanessa's Lady in Waiting. "Thank you for the generous offer, Your Majesty, but I think I'd rather serve as one of Queen Tabitha's maids."

"Very well young lady, you shall have you wish granted," the King chuckled

Chapter Thirteen

Rewarding Results

*O*h reader, you can't imagine how wonderful the next few days went! I had been given my job back, with the firm approval of Miss Primpette, and Mother and Phillip along with all of my friends were told the good news!

When I explained to Mother how everything worked out, she hugged me tight with tears of joy, whispering in my ear over and over, "I knew you could do it. I'm so proud of you Jacqueline!"

I'm not quite sure how well Phillip understood, but he thought it was the most amazing thing on earth to be nearly shot at by a bad guy and then arrest him! In his eyes, I had become a great hero.

From than day on, he was constantly asking me to play swords and knights with him after dinner.

For family devotions, we were on the final chapter of Esther.

I listened peacefully as Mother read verses of how Esther's courage made history! In verses 27-30 it reads, "The Jews took it upon themselves to establish the custom that they and their descendants and all who join them should without fail observe these two days every year, in the way prescribed and at the time appointed.

'These days should be remembered and observed in every generation by every family, and in every province and in every city. And these days of Purim should never cease to be celebrated by the Jews, nor should the memory of them die out among their descendants.

'So Queen Esther, daughter of Abihail, along with Mordecai the Jew, wrote with full authority to confirm this second letter concerning Purim.

'And Mordecai sent letters to all the Jews in the 127 provinces of the kingdom of Xerxes - words of goodwill and assurance."

"Esther reminds me of Jacqueline, mommy," Phillip remarked as the Bible was closed.

Mother looked at me with a twinkle in her eye, "I think that is a very good portrayal, Phillip."

I smiled.

"And now," Mother began taking out a folded sheet of paper from her apron pocket, "I have a special treat for both of you."

I looked over with amusement as Phillip's eyes grew wide and his cute little mouth formed into an oval of surprise. "What is it mommy! What is it!!"

I was excited too, "Yes Mom, what is it?"

"It is a letter from Enrique."

My heart nearly leaped out of my chest! It had been such a long time since we had heard from him. Enrique's regiment had been stationed in the Asian settlement to keep the peace while Lydonians tried to make diplomatic contact with the natives. I missed my older brother very dearly! Before Enrique had gone into the military, he had been my closest friend and confident. What I would give to have him beside me right now! He always encouraged me to do the right thing and would pick me up if I failed. His strength in God was one of the primary reasons that led me to the Savior and kept our family's head above water when father died.

As I sat there in my cottage living room, my heart brimming with joy as Mother opened the letter to read.

Mother cleared her throat,

"My Most Dear, Precious Family,

Forgive the lateness of my letter. I have been trying to send one for quite a while, but it has been rather hectic around here. The settlers do not like the way the Asians are communicating. It. . . . . .well, I won't bother you with details. Feuds can be long, awful things. I am not injured or anything of the sort and in perfect health and condition. I received your letter and am pleased to know all of you are the same as me. You cannot begin to imagine how much I miss you! Sometimes, when I lay on my mat at night, a desperate longing overtakes me to be with all of you once again. To taste Mother's home-cooked pies, to talk with Jacqueline, and to play knights and dragons with Phillip. It makes my smile to think of how much Jacqueline and Phillip will have grown by the time I return! I bet when I come home, Jacqueline will be married with five children and Phillip would have graduated school. Is Jacqueline annoyed with my predictions? I can just imagine her face. By the way, has Phillip started school yet? Have you been able to pay for it? These questions have pestered me for quite some time. I wish I could give you the money Phillip, but alas, a soldier's salary is not a king's. It is hot and muggy out today, but my spirit stays refreshed with the Word of God. He has revealed to me new things every day! How deep, how great, how endless is his love for us! Well, I must take my leave now, the sergeant has summoned me. I will write more in my next letter. I send all of my heart to you, and hope to join you soon! May God protect, strengthen, comfort, and bless you all!

My Deepest Love,
Enrique Richard Noble

Mother's eyes were moist with tears when she finished. She blinked them away hastily and looked at us with a smile. "So, what did you think?"

"I think Enrique should come here right now," Phillip said with a quiet moan.

"It was a beautiful letter," I replied. "I could hear his voice through every word."

All three of us sat there in the still silence for a few moments.

Phillip gave a big yawn and mother stood from the rocking chair. "Well, it's bedtime. Come on Phil."

"But I'm not tired," he protested rubbing his eyes.

"Well, I am. Let's go now," Mother replied gently.

She carried Phillip (who was now sleeping on her shoulder) slowly up the stairs.

I got up from the floor and stretched. It had been a long day. I trudged passed the dying fire in the fireplace and up to my bedroom. Opening the door to my room I beheld the soft moonlight streaming in from the window across the wooden floor. It was a familiar sight, and I smiled. There certainly is no place like home. My eyes were becoming droopy with sleep and the warm covers of my bed were a welcome sight.

I undressed and slipped into my nightgown and hopped into the soft sheets. My gaze rested out of my window and onto the quiet, sloping hills. Little fireflies blinked their light as stars glimmered in the deep blanket of night.

"Thank you Lord, for giving me the courage to do the right thing. Be with Enrique as he is over in a foreign country, dealing with messy affairs. Protect him, and thank you for protecting me. You're so great and good to me! Bless my family and friends, especially Lin - help her to see the truth.

Make my recent experience an example of your faithfulness. Goodnight."

Just as I closed my eyes, Mother entered the room and came to lie on the bed beside me. "Phillip's asleep."

"Soon, I will be too," I replied with a smile.

Mother laughed, "I used to have such trouble getting you to sleep when you were little."

"Not anymore."

Mother smiled and stroked my hair, "No. You're growing up fast, Jacqueline. But you'll always be my little girl."

The next day, I was up in Carlos' stable loft eating lunch

"Tell us again why Jacob Monroe kidnapped Princess Vanessa," Carlos asked me eagerly.

Those present were Mr. Fairday, Lin, Carlos, Roger Steadfast and his sister Rose. They had all assembled here to hear my classic tale.

"Carlos, this is the third time you've heard it," I said with a laugh.

"I know, but Roger and Rose got here late, so they have to hear the details, right?"

"It's okay Carlos, we don't have to. . ." Rose began, but the Spaniard interrupted her. . .

"Nonsense! They *want* to hear it Jacqueline, so tell them."

So, I repeated for the third time in a row, the whole story and for the third time, received applause.

"I am very proud of you little lady," Mr. Fairday said, "you did a wonderful job."

I laughed, "I'm just glad it's over."

"I can't believe the Princess was so ungrateful," Rose said in her sweet voice.

Carlos grunted, "Believe it Rose, she may look nice, I mean, really nice – like the prettiest girl you could ever see on the face of the earth. . . ."

"Carlos!" I interjected.

"But," he finished, "she is a horrible witch when you get to know her."

The quiet, discerning Roger gave a slight smile, "I would imagine she is rather jealous of Jacqueline."

Lin nodded her head in consent to this.

"You are all great fun, but I have to return to work. Ever since Miss Primpette gave me my job back, I've tried to never be missing when work needs to be done."

"Well spoken Miss Noble. And on that note, I will bid you children adieu as well," Mr. Fairday said as he rose.

"We're glad you stayed Jacqueline," Lin replied.

I laughed, "Me too."

Roger and Rose's father had arrived to take them, and so the party dispersed.

Lin and I returned to our work in the east wing. It was our chore to clean Queen Tabitha's bedroom. I set to about shaking the bed sheets and opening the curtains while Lin collected any trash and threw it away.

"Lin," I began, "are you alright?"

"Of course, why do you ask?"

"Well, you were so solemn and quiet up in the loft. Are you sick?"

"No, I'm fine, thank you."

I went back to work, knowing that something was on her mind.

The day was bright and beautiful, the sun shining through the fluffy clouds! I couldn't wait to finish work and then go outside!

Motivated by this, I finished cleaning the Queen's room and was about to walk out the door when I heard Lin ask timidly, "Jacqueline?"

I stopped and turned around, "Yes?"

"I. . .I just wanted to say that, what you did was pretty amazing. I know I could have never done anything like it."

"Oh Lin, I'm not all that, really. I was scared out of my mind!"

"Then how did you do it?" she asked earnestly.

I paused, "Well, God helped me. That's the only solution that comes to my mind."

Lin seemed a bit nervous as she continued, "So, you think God cares about our individual needs?"

I looked at her in some surprise, "Absolutely. He cares about every little thing about you Lin. He *loves* you."

"Do you think he could love me? A child born out of wedlock?"

I leaned against the doorway, my hands beginning to quiver as I sensed what was happening. "He is not willing that any should perish, but all to come to repentance," I quoted. "He *made* you Lin - fashioned you before you were even born. He *died* for you. More than anything else he wants to have a relationship with you. In His Word, the Bible, it says that whoever will confess with his mouth, and believe in his heart that Jesus is Lord, and that God raised him from the dead, he shall be saved."

A pause of silence fell on us.

"Could you show me? How to accept Jesus, I mean," Lin asked shyly.

My heart was beating as I walked towards her. I stuttered my answer, "Yes. . .of course."

We both knelt down on the floor, hand in hand, bowing our heads.

"Just. . .repeat after me," I said with a little tremble.

Lin nodded her head.

"Dear Jesus, I believe that you are Lord. I believe that you died on the cross to save me from my sins. I believe God raised you from the dead. Please, forgive my sins, and enter into my heart. Thank you for loving me so much. Help me to love others the way you love me. Thank you for hearing my prayer, in your name Lord, Amen."

"Amen," Lin finished as tears slipped down her cheeks.

We both looked at each other.

I was far too happy to even speak!

No words were said, for the moment was too wonderful for both of us.

When we finally stood up I looked at Lin and smiled, "Well, Lin Chang. . .welcome to the family!"

To Be Continued. . . .

CPSIA information can be obtained
at www.ICGtesting.com
Printed in the USA
FFOW03n0645050314

4044FF

9 781626 971134